Praise for *The Impatient*

"Djaïli Amadou Amal's words are a tool for liberation. . . . *The Impatient* breaks the silence surrounding forced marriage."

—*Le Monde*

"Bravely exploring the abuse, hardships, and weight of tradition so many women and girls of her region face, Djaïli Amadou Amal's rousing and powerful voice carries a persistent strength that renders their resolve to build a better life all the more moving."

—Cheryl Toman, department chair and professor of French at the University of Alabama, and author of *Contemporary Matriarchies in Cameroonian Francophone Literature*

"[*The Impatient*'s] real complexity lies in its finely textured depictions of relationships between women—mother and daughter, co-wives, sisters—full of jealousy, compassion, and emotional energy."

—*Kirkus Reviews*

"Once opened, *The Impatient* is unputdownable. . . . A deeply moving story imbued with sweeping relevance."

—*La Croix*

"A stark and unflinching view of an oppressive culture."

—*Publishers Weekly*

"Splendidly written . . . *The Impatient* shuttles us through its careening rapids and eddies, keeping us afloat by an unflappable hope."

—*Marie Claire*

"This powerful debut explores what happens when three Cameroonian women dare to challenge tradition, deconstruct taboos, and fight for security and freedom." —*Ms.* magazine

"This is a moving testimony of sheer pain amongst these three women and also a call for change." —Boston.com

The Impatient

The Impatient

A Novel

Djaïli Amadou Amal

Translated from the French by Emma Ramadan

HarperVia

An Imprint of HarperCollinsPublishers

HarperCollins books may be purchased for educational, business, or sales promotional use. For information, please email the Special Markets Department at SPsales@harpercollins.com.

Originally published as *Les Impatientes* in France in 2020 by Éditions Emmanuelle Collas.

FIRST HARPERCOLLINS PAPERBACK PUBLISHED IN 2023

Designed by Terry McGrath

Library of Congress Cataloging-in-Publication Data is available upon request.

ISBN 978-0-06-314164-3

23 24 25 26 27 LBC 5 4 3 2 1

To my husband, Hamadou Baba, and
to all our children, love and tenderness.

Munyal defan hayre.
Patience can cook a stone.

FULANI PROVERB

Contents

RAMLA

*A heart's patience
is proportional
to its grandeur.*

ARAB PROVERB

I

P atience, my girls! *Munyal!* That is the most valuable component of marriage and of life. That is the true value of our religion, of our customs, of *pulaaku*—our Fulani identity. Incorporate patience into your future life. Inscribe it in your heart, repeat it in your mind! *Munyal*, don't forget it!" my father says. His voice is serious.

Head lowered, I am drowning in emotion. My aunts have brought Hindou and I into our father's apartment. Outside, the effervescence of the double wedding is in full swing. The cars are already parked. The in-laws are waiting, impatient. The children, excited by the festivities, shout and dance around the cars. Our friends and younger sisters, unaware of our anguish, stand by our sides. They envy us, dreaming of the day when they will be the queens of the party. The griots are here, accompanied by lute and tambourine players. They sing words of praise at the top of their lungs in honor of the family and the new sons-in-law.

My father is seated on his favorite sofa. He calmly sips a cup of clove tea. Hayatou and Oumarou, my uncles, are also present, surrounded by a few close friends. These men are supposed to pass on their final words of advice, list our future duties as wives, and then say their goodbyes—after granting us their blessings.

"*Munyal*, my girls, for patience is a virtue. God loves those who are patient," my father repeats, imperturbable. "Today I have achieved my duty as your father. I raised you, instructed you, and today I entrust you to these responsible men! You are now big girls—women! Henceforth you are married and owe respect and consideration to your husbands."

I adjust my coat around me. It's a sumptuous *alkibbare*. I am sitting next to my sister Hindou at our father's feet on a bright red Turkish rug that contrasts sharply with our dark dresses. We are surrounded by our aunts who, designated as our elder *kamo*, fulfill the role of maids of honor. As with every marriage, Goggo Nenné, Goggo Diya, and their acolytes have enormous difficulty masking their emotion. Only their sniffling disturbs the silence. Tears dig deep grooves in their wrinkled cheeks. They don't attempt to hide their red eyes. Through us, they relive their own weddings. They, too, were brought to their fathers for a final goodbye and received the customary advice passed down from generation to generation with each new bride.

"*Munyal*, my girls!" says my uncle Hayatou. Then he pauses and clears his throat before listing orders in a solemn tone:

> Respect your five daily prayers.
> Read the Quran so that your progeny will be blessed.
> Fear your God.
> Spare your minds from distraction.
> Be for him a slave and he will be your captive.

Be for him the earth and he will be your sky.

Be for him a field and he will be your rain.

Be for him a bed and he will be your hut.

Do not sulk.

Do not look down on a gift, do not return it.

Do not be bad-tempered.

Do not be talkative.

Do not be scatter-brained.

Do not beg, do not demand.

Be modest.

Be grateful.

Be patient.

Be discreet.

Valorize him so that he will honor you.

Respect his family and submit to them so that they
    will support you.

Aid your husband.

Preserve his fortune.

Preserve his dignity.

Preserve his appetite.

May he never starve because of your laziness, your
    bad mood, or your bad cooking.

Spare his sight, his hearing, his sense of smell.

May his eyes never be confronted by anything dirty
    in your food or in your house.

May his ears never hear obscenities or insults coming
    from your mouth.

May his nose never smell anything that reeks in your

body or in your house, may he breathe in only
perfume and incense.

These words lodge in my mind. I feel my heart break, realizing
that my worst nightmare is coming to life.

Up to the last minute, naively, I had hoped that a miracle
would spare me from this hardship. A powerless, mute rage stran-
gles me. A desire to smash everything, to cry, to scream. My sister
stops holding back her tears and sobs. Suffocates. I reach for her
hand and squeeze it to comfort her. Faced with her distress, I feel
strong despite my pain. Now that I am being separated from her,
Hindou is all the more dear to me.

"May your parents never learn of anything unpleasant in your
household. Keep your conjugal conflicts to yourself—do not cultivate dislike between your two families, for you will reconcile but
the hatred you sow will last," adds Uncle Hayatou.

After a moment of silence, my father continues in the same
solemn and authoritative tone:

"Starting now, you each belong to your husband and owe him
total submission, as decreed by Allah. Without his permission,
you do not have the right to leave the house or even to visit my
bedside. Only by following this rule will you be successful wives!"

Uncle Oumarou, who had kept quiet up to this point, continues:

"Always remember: To please her husband, every time they
meet, a wife must perfume herself with her most precious perfume, adorn herself in her most beautiful attire, ornament herself
with jewelry—and much more! A woman's paradise is at her husband's feet."

He pauses as if to give us time to reflect, then turns toward his younger brother and concludes:

"Hayatou, complete the *do'a*, speak the prayer. May Allah grant them happiness, honor their household with numerous children, and give them the *baraka*. Finally, may Allah grant every father the joy of seeing his daughter married!"

"Amine!" my father responds. Then he addresses my aunts: "Go now. The cars are waiting."

Goggo Nenné elbows me. In a muffled voice, I thank my father, then my uncles. To everyone's surprise, Hindou throws herself in tears at the feet of our stunned father and begs:

"Please, Baaba, listen to me: I don't want to marry him! Please, let me stay here."

"What is this nonsense, Hindou?"

"I don't love Moubarak!" she says, sobbing even harder. "I don't want to marry him."

My father barely glances at the teenager hunched at his feet. Turning toward me, he orders calmly:

"Go! May Allah grant them happiness."

And it's over. That's the only goodbye I receive from my father, whom I will probably not see again for another year—if everything goes according to plan.

At that moment, despite the distance that has always existed between us, I wanted my father to speak to me, to tell me he was going to miss me. I hoped he would assure me of his love, murmur that I would always be his little girl, that this house would always be mine and that I would still be welcome here. But I know that such things are unrealistic. We aren't in one of those foreign TV series that inspired our teenage dreams, nor in one of those soppy novels that so delighted us. We are neither the first nor the last girls that my father and uncles will marry off. On the contrary, they are content to have seamlessly accomplished their duty. Since our childhood, they have waited for this moment when they could finally offload their responsibilities by entrusting us, still virgins, to other men.

My aunts lead us, completely veiled, toward the exit. There are so many women waiting for us in the large courtyard that my hand loses Hindou's. I cannot say a word to her. Already, amid the ululation, I am brought to the car awaiting me. A final glance and I see her, in tears, distraught. She is shoved into the second car.

II

For the whole drive, per the custom, I am accompanied by shouts of joy. The luxurious black Mercedes I'm sitting in advances ahead of dozens of others, horns blaring. The procession drives around the city before entering a magnificent compound gleaming with colorful lights. The sounds of tom-toms and the songs of griots blend with the youyous of overexcited women and children, creating an incredible cacophony.

An hour later, my co-wife comes to welcome me. I stare at her from beneath my veil. Contrary to how I had imagined her, she is not old. She is in the prime of her thirties, a woman of great beauty.

I hope to ally myself with her, but the look she gives me forbids it. She seems to detest me before even knowing me. She, too, is surrounded by the women of her family, who all display polite smiles.

The two camps stare each other down, scrutinizing each other in a tacit duel, barely concealing a honeyed contempt.

My co-wife is dressed like a bride. A sparkling pagne wrapper, her beautiful braids, hands and feet decorated with henna. But I can tell that she's making an enormous effort to remain calm. Her lips form a slight smile that does not hide the sadness of her eyes.

They say she sank into depression upon the announcement of this marriage, that she spent entire days crying. She must have come around thanks to the support of her family—or did she simply concede that nothing and no one could dissuade her husband from this marriage that all the city was mocking?

Her eyes examine me, pierce through me. Our gazes meet. And the hatred I read in hers makes me lower mine.

My eldest sister-in-law, highly regarded by other women, addresses my co-wife:

"My dear Safira, here is the new bride, your *amariya*. Her name is Ramla. She is your younger sister, your little one, your daughter. Her family entrusts her to you. You must help her now, by passing down your advice, by showing her the ways of the compound. You are the first wife, the *daada-saaré*. And, as you know, the *daada-saaré* is the guide of the house, the one who ensures the harmony of the home.

"*Daada-saaré*, you will also be the punching bag of the house. You will keep your place as *daada-saaré* even if your husband marries ten others. So, a single word: *munyal*, patience! For everything depends on you. You are the pillar of the house. It's up to you to make the effort, to be resilient and conciliatory. In order to be so, you will have to practice perfect self-control from now on. *Munyal*. You, Safira, the *daada-saaré*, *jiddere-saaré*, the mother, the mistress of the home and the punching bag of the household! *Munyal, munyal* . . ."

Then she turns toward me:

"Ramla, you are now Safira's little sister, her daughter, and she is your mother. You owe her obedience and respect. You will entrust yourself to her, ask her advice, follow her orders. You are the younger sister. You will not take any initiative to do with the management of the compound without the approval of your *daada-saaré*. She is the mistress of the house. You are only her little sister. Your job is the thankless tasks. Absolute obedience, patience before her anger, respect! *Munyal, munyal . . .*"

We listen in silence, nodding our heads in a sign of acquiescence. Then Safira leaves, accompanied by her family. My own leaves soon after. Only the women who, according to custom, have been chosen to accompany me for the first days of the marriage remain. They settle into my new apartment, located just opposite that of my co-wife. And Goggo Nenné has the honor of leading me into the bridal chamber.

III

I grew up in a Fulani household, similar to all the other afflu-ent compounds in Maroua, in northern Cameroon. My father, Alhadji Boubakari, belongs to the generation of Fulani who left their native village and came to live in the town, thus diversifying their opportunities. Today he is a businessman, as are his brothers. However, he kept in Danki, his home village, a herd of oxen that he entrusted to the shepherds who still practice traditional trans-humance. For the ox is the symbol of the Fulani. And my family is not the exception to the rule.

At a lively sixty years old, my father is a handsome man. Dig-nified in all circumstances, always impeccably dressed, he wears a starched *gandoura* and a matching cap.

Custom imposes restraint in parent-child relations to the point where it is impossible to show any emotion or sentiment. This is why he is not particularly close to his children. The sole proof I have of his paternal love is that I exist. I don't know whether my father ever carried me in his arms or held my hand. He always kept an insurmountable distance from his daughters, and it never occurred to me to complain. That was just how things were. Only the boys could see my father more often, enter his apartment, eat with him, and sometimes even accompany him to the market or to the mosque. On the other hand, they could not linger inside the compound, which was the domain of women. Muslim society defined a place for each sex.

We are a large family. My father presides over us with an iron fist. Four wives gave him thirty children, of which the eldest, mostly girls, are married. Baaba does not tolerate conflict, and so each of his wives keeps quiet about any little incidents or disputes that might trouble the polygamous household. Our large family exists in a seemingly harmonious, serene atmosphere.

Our compound is surrounded by three high walls that keep anyone from seeing inside; it shelters my father's domain. Visitors never see that area; they are received at the entrance in a vestibule that, in the tradition of Fulani hospitality, is called the *zawleru*. Behind it is an immense space with several buildings: first the imposing villa of my father, the patriarch, then the *hangar*, a sort of portico under which guests are received, and finally the dwellings of the wives, where the men do not enter. To speak to her husband, a wife must seek the permission of the co-wife whose turn it is.

My five uncles live in the same neighborhood. We have not one but six compounds. And, if we add to my father's thirty children those of all the family combined, there are easily more than eighty children in total. We, the daughters, live with our respective mothers while our brothers have their own rooms away from the maternal apartments starting at a young age. And, of course, girls and boys only cross paths, hardly speaking to each other.

With her light, slightly bronzed skin, her chestnut eyes, and her silky, pitch-black hair, peppered with a few grays and falling to her shoulders in beautiful, regularly refreshed braids, my mother is still a very beautiful woman despite her dozen pregnancies. Barely fifty, with her ample curves graciously dressed in vibrantly colored pagnes, she sways her hips with each step in a movement of stirring sensuality. She is my father's first wife and totally submissive to him. When he decides to take a new wife, hypocritically she wishes her all the happiness in the world, praying that the newcomer will not last long. When he repudiates one of them, she shows compassion and takes care of the unfortunate woman's children. She is my father's lucky charm. As soon as they were married, his business started booming. It is generally believed that the lucky star of his spouse determines a man's prosperity. But the esteem she enjoys does not spare her from her husband's bellicose moods and does not guarantee her better treatment. Her ability to keep her place simply comes down to her patience. She has the fortunate ability to accept everything, to endure everything, and, above all, to forget everything . . . or to pretend!

But, in private, my mother spends her time wallowing in bitterness. Today she is more bitter than usual, experiencing a terrible feeling of failure. She has a harder time tolerating the disputes and low blows that spice up life in the compound. Alternately, she blames her three co-wives, whose children are intolerably insolent, of taking years off her life. She laments the unemployment of her eldest sons and regrets the bad marriages of her daughters, for which she reproaches her husband deep down. She finds it unjust but has no desire to end up repudiated. A matter of self-preservation!

IV

I am different. I always was. To my mother, I seemed like an alien. While my sisters swooned over colorful pagnes that our father's employee brought each year for the celebration at the end of Ramadan, fighting to claim the color that best suited, I would arrive well behind everyone else, take the pagne that no one else wanted, and leave, bored, to plunge back into my books. While my sisters discontinued their studies as early as possible, not wanting to disobey my father, and agreed to marry the men that he or one of my uncles chose for them (they were more interested in the material aspects of marriage, the gifts or the interior design of their future home), I stubbornly persisted in going to high school.

I explained to the women of the family my ambition to become a pharmacist, which made them burst into laughter. They called me crazy and bragged about the virtues of marriage and the life of a homemaker.

When I doubled down on the fulfillment that a woman could find in the pleasure of having a job, driving her car, or managing her property, they abruptly cut off the conversation, advising me sharply to come back down to earth, to reality.

For them, the greatest possible joy was to marry a rich man who would shelter them from need, offer them pagnes and jewels and a house full of trinkets and—most important—maids. An idle life spent amid the four walls of a beautiful compound. For a successful marriage is measured by the number of gold jewels worn ostentatiously at every festive opportunity. And a woman's happiness is achieved through her travels to Mecca and Dubai, through her numerous children and her beautiful interior decoration. The best husband is not the one who cherishes, but the one who protects and is generous. It is inconceivable that things could be otherwise.

To the great displeasure of my mother, certain that only marriage was suitable for a woman, and to the total indifference of my father, who never knew anything about our activities, I turned out to be very gifted.

It was one of my father's employees who kept track of our studies, at least those of the children whose mothers had been vigilant and open enough to require it. "Kept track" is a bit of a stretch. He was content simply to enroll the youngest in school and buy the supplies we needed. Whether we moved up a grade or had to repeat a year didn't matter to him, since it also didn't matter to anyone in the family. Only my father's latest conquest cared, for she was also the only one to have attended high school.

My brothers and sisters all stopped going to school when they encountered the slightest difficulty: a bad grade, a repeat year, a disagreement with a teacher. And it elicited no comment from our parents. That was in fact the fate of all the young people in the city. The boys ended up assisting my father or my uncles in their stores, where they learned the shopkeeping trade on the job. As for the girls, they stayed home, dolling themselves up, reading the Quran, and patiently waiting for our father to find them a husband. The luckiest, which is to say the prettiest, who thus had the most suitors, could choose for themselves—on condition that the man met Baaba's expectations, of course.

I am seventeen years old and in my final year of general science. As of now, I am the most educated of my sisters. Only my brother Amadou, at university, is still pursuing his studies and stubbornly refuses to join the family business. My father, out of desperation, tells himself that he'll be a scholar—or even a civil servant—and that it will be good to have one in the family.

We wear a uniform in all the middle and high schools in the city, but like all the Muslim women, in case I cross paths with a man of the family on the way, I wear a pagne over my uniform and cover my head with a scarf that I remove upon entering the school. Since fifth grade, I've watched my friends and classmates get married one after another. In primary school, there were fifty of us; now there are only ten. But for me, as for the others, it's just a matter of time. A crowd of suitors has courted me since I was thirteen. I am considered beautiful in our country. Light, almost pale skin, silky and long hair, delicate features. Invariably, when a man asks for my hand, I tell him to wait. Always the same response, a litany.

"Yes, I want to marry you, but not right away! I'm still in school, you see. Maybe in two or three years . . ."

Custom forbids girls from rejecting a suitor. Even if we are not interested, we must nevertheless avoid offending a man.

Invariably, they reply:

"Two years! But you'll be an old girl by then, my pretty. What use is it for you to pass the baccalaureate? The most important thing for a girl is to be married. I'm in too much of a rush to wait two years. You're not thinking clearly. I'll go to see your father and ask for your hand."

"I'm asking for a bit of time to reflect."

"Ah! You're saying that because you don't like me!"

I want to shout: "How could I like you? I don't even know you. And I don't want to know you."

But, since I'm a well-educated girl who knows her *pulaaku* like the back of her hand, I lower my eyes timidly and respond:

"I do! Of course I like you, but I still want to wait a bit."

All this makes my mother's blood boil.

"Are you crazy, Ramla? You're out of your mind. If that's what they teach you in school, you won't be going back. What's wrong with that one? Why did you refuse him? What shame! What a curse! You've been bewitched! My word, what misfortune! Your little sister Hindou will be married before you. What shame, my God! Have you no pity for your poor mother? Do you want Hindou's mother, your stepmother, to mock me even more? A man so young and so well off! What's gotten into you? What are you looking for exactly? You've refused the younger ones and the older ones, the rich and the civil servants—even the monogamists! I should tell your father to set you up. In fact, keep this up and you won't have the luxury to choose your husband. Your father or one of your uncles will gladly take care of it for you . . ."

This continues for a long time. My mother never stops lamenting, desperate to make me hear reason. She calls my older brothers and married sisters as witnesses. She complains to my aunts. And all of them persist for days and days in trying to convince me. The newcomer always has all the desirable virtues. He's the best choice for me.

One day, to everyone's surprise, I did not refuse. His name was Aminou. He was my brother Amadou's best friend. He often came to the house. And we hit it off. He was the only boy I spoke to without suffering the reprisals of my brothers, who had proclaimed themselves our protectors. He was studying telecommunications in Tunisia and hoped to become an engineer. When his father asked for my hand, my father found no reason to say no. My mother was ecstatic, I had shown no resistance. Finally! And for me, it was like a dream come true. Soon, he and I would be married. Soon, in a few years, at the University of Tunis, he would become an engineer and I would become a pharmacist. We would be happy. Far from everything. Far from here!

V

My dreams were short-lived. When Uncle Hayatou informed my father that their most important business partner had asked for my hand and he had granted it, my father not only accepted but thanked him warmly. Hayatou, the richest of the brothers, watched over the family's well-being, and for that he was respected. My father would never have thought to oppose his brother's decision, even concerning one of his own children. I was not just my father's daughter. I was the daughter of all the family. And each of my uncles could manage me as their own child. It was out of the question for me to disagree. I was their daughter. I had been raised according to tradition, taught the strict respect that I owed my elders.

My mother was tasked with breaking the news. I had noticed during the night that she was preoccupied by some worry. She waited until late at night, when the compound was plunged into darkness, to gently awaken me. She didn't want our conversation to fall on indiscreet ears. Her co-wives, dogged rivals, were always waiting for an occasion to point out her weaknesses. They couldn't know that she or one of her children was having an issue. She also couldn't rouse their jealousy, at risk of sending them rushing to the nearest marabout to undermine this new blessing.

The gravity of her expression made me fear the worst. I sat up immediately.

"Mother, what's going on?"

"Nothing bad, quite the opposite. Nothing but happiness! *Al-hamdulillah!* Your good fortune awakens. Finally, I can lift my head with pride, and it's thanks to you. Finally, my dignity is solidified. But I am not surprised. I knew you would have an exceptional life."

"What do you mean?"

"Your uncle Hayatou granted your hand to another. You won't be marrying Aminou. Your father wanted you to know."

"Who is it?"

"Alhadji Issa! The most important man in town. You're trading up. My only concern is that he already has a wife. I would have preferred to spare you from polygamy. I suffer from it every day. But, in any event, if you don't find a woman upon entering your home, another one will catch up to you sooner or later. Better to find one than wait around for another! A new bride who will make more than one person pale with envy and jealousy in this wolves' den. I already have to protect you from those witches, your stepmothers."

"But Diddi, I don't even know him!"

"He knows you. Apparently, he absolutely insisted on marrying you. Your father is very proud, you know."

"But I love Aminou! He's the one I want to marry."

"Love doesn't exist before marriage, Ramla. It's time you come back down to earth. We're not white. We're not Hindu either. Now you understand why your father didn't want you all to watch those TV shows! You will do what your father and your uncles tell you. You don't have a choice. Spare yourself from useless worry, my girl.

Spare me, too. Don't kid yourself, the slightest disobedience on your part will inevitably come back to bite me."

She continued for a long time in this tone, drying her eyes occasionally, while I cried frantically, stifling the sound of my sobs in the folds of my pagne.

"There's no use getting so worked up. You are lucky, and I am, too. Trust in my experience as a woman. You are too young to understand the importance of such an alliance. Marriage isn't just about love. The most important thing for a woman is to be sheltered from need. Protected, idolized.

"Your potential husband is first and foremost the father of your future children. You have to be mindful of his nobility, his family, his comportment, his social status. So dry your eyes and go back to bed.

"Pray to Allah. He is opening the best doors for you. And, above all, do not show the slightest sign of disappointment in the presence of the other women of the family. If your destiny is to marry him, you will not escape it. And if your destiny is to marry another, you won't change anything on that front either. Everything is in the hands of the Creator. Pray that He grant you the best outcome."

A few days after this announcement, my uncle Hayatou called me to meet this man who had apparently noticed me among the school procession on Youth Day and had decided to make me his second wife. He entered my uncle's living room, cavalier. Dressed in a rich *gandoura* with flashy embroidery, he was opulence incarnate. He never stopped smiling and stared at me shamelessly. I sat far from him, at the very edge of the rug, and kept my head lowered. Not once did I lift my eyes to look at him. Alongside my proper education that required I practice restraint was a repressed desire for revolt. I had not chosen him. I wasn't given the chance to accept or refuse him. It was thus pointless whether I liked him or not. This meeting was for his satisfaction alone. For him to be able to look at me as he pleased and confirm his first furtive impressions.

I kept quiet and didn't answer his questions. It would certainly take a lot more than that to dampen his enthusiasm—he spoke enough for us both!

"All those young men courting you," he began, "are nothing but lowlifes. They drink, they smoke, they take drugs. With me you'll be an important woman and you'll have everything you desire. Here's an idea! I'll take you to Mecca this year and, since you're educated, you'll come with me on my next trip to Europe. We'll be married quickly. I would have liked to be married even sooner but I understand you want to finish the school year. You're in your final year, that's very good! You're an intellectual that I can bring with me to official ceremonies. You'll make me proud, how wonderful!"

He continued his monologue for a long time. He didn't ask my opinion. It was unthinkable to him that I wouldn't want to marry him.

Yes, that would have been inconceivable.

What girl would refuse such an important man? It was a done deal. He had discussed it with my uncle. The rest was just a formality.

VI

My father, embarrassed by the turn of events—he didn't like to go back on his word—informed Aminou's family.

"Destiny decided otherwise," he claimed.

Magnanimous, he offered Aminou the choice of another of his daughters. Zaytouna! My half sister was just a few years younger than me. Or Jamila! Yes, my sister from the same mother. She was a year younger, and we looked as similar as two drops of water. Why not her? Or else any of my uncles' daughters. There were still a dozen left to marry . . .

Scandalized and mad with rage, Aminou firmly rejected the proposition of an exchange. Accompanied by his friend Amadou, as disappointed as he was, he insisted on seeing our father to convince him to reverse his decision.

As soon as my father caught sight of the young men, he grimaced, agitated, then addressed them:

"Tell me, Aminou. You've been harassing me for days—with the complicity of my own son on top of it. I already said what I had to say to you. Do you think you'll change my mind by behaving this way? I offered you another of my daughters. Pick one before I change my mind. You're bringing shame to your father and to your whole family."

"I don't want any of your other daughters. I asked for Ramla's hand and you gave it to me. I did nothing wrong for you to go back on your word."

"My brother had already given her hand to another. Destiny had other plans in mind, that's all."

"Ramla and I agreed on it."

"Ramla is a girl. And she is well raised. She will marry who we tell her to marry."

"But come on, Baaba," Amadou interrupted. "The world has changed! Girls have the right . . ."

"Get out of my sight, you insolent child! I know what you're up to. You better watch out, Amadou! You must have a screw loose, talking to me about women's rights! Where is your modesty? Your good education? What are you trying to teach me? On top of it, you dare to contradict me! Such bad manners! Such impudence! Leave now, both of you. I've had enough of this foolishness. Aminou, get this through your head. You will not marry Ramla. Forget about her!"

The young men, aided by a few friends, loudly protested through the entire city, chanting that the old man should be ashamed to contest the engagement of someone younger. They made so much noise that my uncle Hayatou got angry and sent the most boisterous to jail to calm their fervor. Furious at Amadou, who had dared to defy him in public, and fearing that all the tumult would reach Alhadji Issa and disrupt the turn of events, my father summoned my uncles Hayatou and Moussa and had me sit with them in the living room, on the rug, next to my mother, who had also been summoned.

Aware that she had not been called for good news, my mother was so anxious that she seemed to be holding her breath, her lips pursed. My father, majestic on his sofa, his expression one of implacable coldness, stared at the two of us for a long time before addressing my mother haughtily:

"Dadiyel, it's unlike you to be so disobedient. Why is it that your son dares to embarrass me through the entire city? And your daughter? It seems that she has gone around loudly proclaiming her love for her little lowlife? I hope I am mistaken, Ramla."

I said nothing and lowered my eyes. But I started to cry in silence. He continued:

"Do you dare defy me, you amoral girl? Do you dare humiliate my brother for his generosity in finding you a man when you don't even deserve it?" he asked angrily, raising his voice. "This is what happens when you leave girls in school too long. They think they've grown wings and start to meddle in everything. Marriage is not just a matter of feelings. On the contrary, it's first and foremost an alliance between two families. It's also a question of honor, of responsibility, of religion—and much more."

My father could scarcely mask his anger. He had married off a dozen daughters without a hitch. So my revolt, though discreet, irritated him profoundly. He was even more exasperated because the stakes of this marriage went beyond a simple marital union. He continued, addressing my mother:

"If your daughter or your son utter even a single wrong word again, I will repudiate you. No! On the head of my brothers now present, I will repudiate you three times.* I think I've been more than patient up until now. Do you understand?"

"I beseech you, Alhadji, it's really not my fault. I tried to reason with the children. They simply don't listen to me."

My uncle, very tense, stood up to add fuel to the fire:

"If they don't listen to their mother, it's because they are cursed children. Ramla, if ever a single negative word about Alhadji Issa comes out of your mouth, I will teach you a lesson in modesty and restraint befitting a well-raised girl. You little ingrate. Have you ever wanted for anything? Who enrolled you in school? Don't you see that with the way you and your low-life friends are acting, you're jeopardizing my business and your father's? And they said you were intelligent. You want us to get hit with high taxes for upsetting that politician? You want our main supplier to stop delivering to us? Perhaps you want to ruin us?"

"No!" I answered in a barely audible voice, feeling my convictions give way.

"Well then, I command you to behave like a dignified girl. Tonight I'll send my employee with a few catalogues of furniture for you to choose from. I trust you'll cooperate and select the most beautiful things for your future home. I don't want you sulking in front of your future co-wife. I'll buy you all the furniture as your wedding gift. Now you can go."

I left without a word, my mother still curled up in a corner. Behind me, I heard my father and uncle reproaching her. She would be the one to pay for all of our missteps. It was the worst

---

* Repudiating a woman three times translates to divorce with no recourse.

blackmail they could hold against me and my brother Amadou. Checkmate. It was over. I had understood.

Aminou sank into depression. He stopped eating, he stopped washing himself, and he spent his days sunk in an endless melancholy. Frightened at the idea that his son might go mad, his father sent him back to Tunisia. As for Amadou, they ordered him to shut up once and for all, under threat of returning to prison, and not just for a day this time. In any event, he would not risk our mother being repudiated. We are in fact witnesses every day to the injustices suffered by our brothers whose mothers are repudiated, so as not to put our youngest half brothers in the same situation. It was over. Aminou was gone. And I remained. Alone, facing the prospect of marriage to a stranger. Alone with my anguish. Alone with my tears. All I could do now was mourn my lost illusions. And my mother no longer hid her resentment toward Aminou, who had not only strayed from the path of a good son, but also disturbed the mind of her daughter. She invented every fault for him. He was a skirt chaser and, of course, he drank and smoked. Suddenly, Alhadji Issa possessed every good quality. He was rich, I would have everything I desired. He was a politician, I would be respected and highly regarded. He was older, I would be able to manipulate him even better. He had a wife and children, he would be more serious. All day long, all anyone spoke about was my imminent wedding. I was harassed by everyone. Never in all my life had I felt so alone. The vise tightened around me. No one bothered to ask whether I was happy or not. The only thing that mattered to them was the extraordinary ceremony that went along with any wedding worthy of the name. Excitement gripped every neighborhood of the city. I was the new idol of Maroua. The most coveted of the girls. I had driven wild with love a man known for his riches, his rigor, and his high standards for women. I had even managed to turn that unwavering monogamist polygamous. And, the most miraculous of all, I had been able to distract him from his fierce and possessive wife, who, rumor had it, was a faithful client of all the marabouts of the city and even beyond. In sum, I was a heroine!

The women of the family spoke of the wedding as of an inescapable duty. And if, by a stroke of misfortune, I happened to mention love, they called me crazy, told me I was egotistical and childish, that I lacked heart and had no sense of dignity. I was beautiful; it wasn't up to me to run toward my future husband. It was instead up to him to do everything to earn me. My aunt repeated to me every day:

"Don't marry the one you love. If you want to be happy, marry the one who loves you!"

No one threatened me anymore. There was nothing left to say now. They expected me to be dignified and to yield to our traditions. I wasn't even a problem anymore. I had to obey, that's all there was to it. Neither my father nor my uncle thought to say anything to me. They had simply set a date. The date that would chain me for life.

Goggo Nenné was the one to tell me.

I didn't cry, I didn't retaliate. I was already dead inside. I was lucky, she said to me, smiling. The list of suitors I had turned away was already very long. I had nearly ended up an old maid! It was the custom for a father to choose his daughter's husband.

It had been that way for my six older sisters, for my cousins, for my mother, and even for her, my aunt. I was no different! I had to walk with dignity like all the others before me. Once more, I was lucky. They were allowing me to take my exam. They were giving me the chance to get my degree, even if it would be useless. At least I would be able to say that I had graduated. The wedding would take place immediately after the exam. I was lucky! My father and my fiancé were taking my ambitions into account. I was truly lucky, repeated my aunt Nenné.

My wedding date was set for the upcoming break, the same day as my sister Hindou's wedding to Moubarak, our cousin. Meanwhile, I could continue to go to school and prepare for my exam.

VII

The wedding date set, I spent all day wallowing in a laziness and a silence that nothing and no one could break. I stopped eating, I stopped laughing. I visibly lost weight. I took my exam with no conviction and learned of my passing with total indifference.

Then the wedding preparations began. A woman came specially from Chad, paid for by my fiancé. She began by waxing me completely. Morning and night, she covers my entire body in *dilké*. Made from potatoes, rice, oil, and intoxicating perfumes, that smelly black wet paste is used as a scrub. After a half hour break, she massages me for a long time before coating my body in a vegetable oil perfumed with clove and yellowed with turmeric. In another context, I might have enjoyed these treatments.

Next, the woman put embers in a receptacle, covered in acacia sticks reserved specially for this purpose, and I had to incense myself for an hour. Wrapped in a thick cover, I sweat an enormous amount in the horrible heat of the improvised sauna, which is supposed to render my skin more luminous and my complexion brighter. A ritual inherited from Sudan via Chad.

Sequestered in my mother's room, I must remain hidden. My jovial esthetician flatters me endlessly:

"Really, Ramla, what a beauty you are! Your skin is getting softer and softer. And your body is fragrant. For months your sweat will continue to smell like acacia and sandalwood. Alhadji Issa won't be able to resist, you'll see. He'll offer you everything a woman might desire. Your co-wife will have a hard time rivaling you! If she even finds the courage to stay. Yes, my girl, it's true. Trust my experience! He'll be like a toy in your hands. You will be happy!"

I don't respond. What can I say to this stranger who praises me like the eighth wonder of the world? For whom marrying a well-to-do man is the height of happiness? How could I make her understand without hurting her that I do not care about this man?

The night before the wedding, she finishes her work by spending an entire day tattooing my arms, my legs, my bust, and my back with black henna. On my light skin, the dark designs create a nice effect. She even incorporates the initials of my future betrothed!

She is not the only one to prepare me for the wedding. My father also takes part—in a different way. He brings, for my bath, bark meant to protect me from the evil eye, *gaadés* supposed to give me charm, incense to protect me from jinns. He asks marabouts to write thousands of Quranic verses on planks that are then washed. And I drink holy water, under the strict surveillance of my mother, to make me more pleasing for this husband I don't want and to protect me from the co-wife being thrust on me.

Two days before the fateful date, I try a last-ditch effort on my mother, who's come to keep me company:

"Diddi, if you force me to marry him, I'll kill myself!"

"If you kill yourself, you'll go straight to hell, and if you continue to sulk, I swear I'll have a fit. I'll die—and it will be your fault. At best, I'll be repudiated. Is that what you want? And it's not just me who's involved. What about your little brothers? Your little sisters? They're too young to live without protection in this wolf's den. Are you prepared to sacrifice them for your own supposed happiness? We're not damning you to hell, Ramla. Quite the opposite. You will marry a man who'll ensure you never lack food or clothing, and you will have more possessions than you could ever desire. Look at your half sister Maïmouna. Her husband barely guarantees the necessities, and she still relies on your father to feed and dress her. Is that how you want to live? I would never let you risk poverty."

"You don't understand, Mother! I mean . . ."

She cuts me off with a wave of her hand, lowering her voice even more. A severe crease wrinkles her still smooth forehead.

"You need to get it into your head once and for all that your decisions have an effect outside of your own life. Grow up, my God! It was the same for me, for your aunts, for all the women in your family. What are you trying to prove? Your younger sisters might not be enrolled in school because of you. You managed to give education a bad name with your behavior. Get ahold of yourself, Ramla. Be grateful for your fate and thank Allah for not handing you a worse destiny. Would you rather marry Moubarak, that loser cousin of yours?"

"Of course not!" I say quietly.

"Because believe me, Hindou's mother would be more than happy for her daughter to marry Alhadji Issa. Why do you want at all costs to humiliate me?"

"I could never humiliate you, Diddi. You're misunderstanding me. I have to accept this marriage, everyone tells me so. But do my feelings not matter? Is anyone thinking about me? I don't want to get married. I wanted to continue my studies."

"You've already finished your studies. If you weren't about to be married, you would be staying at home. Never would your father allow you to go to university. Not here and definitely not anywhere else."

"That's part of why I agreed to marry Aminou. With him, I could have continued. And I love him."

"Well, your love is useless; it holds no power because it's not reciprocated," she says mercilessly. "Cut out your nonsense once and for all or I'll leave you here on your own! Have you no dignity, Ramla? Or have you lost the sense of honor we imparted to you?"

"How do you know whether Aminou loves me or not?"

She bursts into sad laughter:

"If he loves you, as you would like to believe, then answer me this: Where is he?"

VIII

The day before the wedding, Alhadji Issa sent dozens of bags of kola nuts and boxes of candies and sweets for the ceremony, which is called the *tégal*. I haven't slept at all lately. I can't stop wrestling with the same images in my head. The most difficult part is forgetting Aminou. Will I be able to one day? And did I really want to forget him? The memory of him was sharp and sweet. I felt alone. My mother, aware of my distress, wrote it off as childishness and said that as soon as I was married, I would be happier about my fate. But I had to understand that this was my destiny and that "in the face of destiny, we are powerless," she affirmed. Would I not soon be the wife of one of the richest men in the city?

Yes, it was a destiny like every mother dreams of. A destiny that would turn all my mother's co-wives green with envy. As evidenced by my stepmothers' and half sisters' glimmers of longing at the sight of the brand-new car my fiancé gave to me one night as a first wedding gift.

Anxiety tormented me. I couldn't sit still. I was suffocating. I had cried so much that my eyes had turned red, my eyelids were puffed up. This silent despair had not moved my mother or my aunts. They had all cried at their weddings. The tears of a young wife merely reflect her nostalgia for a fleeing youth, for a lost innocence and the responsibilities to come. They express only her attachment to her family and her fear at the idea of moving into a strange house.

Late in the night, tired from dwelling on my bitterness, I suddenly felt the need to leave my austere bedroom. I wanted to see the moon, stare at the stars. Surely I'll see them again from where I'll be, but will they have the same gleam? And the air? Will it be as pure? And the gentle humming of the light wind through the neem leaves? Will it be as charged with that fresh, delicate perfume? And will the sand be as soft beneath my feet?

The whole house was sleeping. My mother had collapsed onto the little mattress in the living room, wiped out by fatigue. Several women were spending the night in the house. Some were asleep on the rug. Fearful of waking them and above all that they might catch me and hold me back, I stepped over them silently.

How should I take advantage of my final hours of freedom? And to think that tomorrow, at this very hour, I'll be forced to share the bed of a stranger. A man who will let his hands run over my skin prepared for his pleasure, ogle the tattoos destined to seduce him, inhale the fragrance of incense, and have the right to possess me entirely, even though I don't love him, even though I love another. How can I accept that I will leave my house and my family to belong to another?

If only it would all be over tomorrow! But marriage is not just a ceremony; it lasts a lifetime.

The night was calm, brisk for the season, and the sky was strewn with thousands of stars. The moon illuminated the city, and it was visible as though by the light of day. I would have preferred a black night, as frightening as this anguish gripping my throat and knotting my stomach. It was over, I could never again go out whenever I so desired, never finish my studies, my dreams of going to university were finished. A prisoner in a luxury cage, I would never be a pharmacist now.

Never had I been so alone.

Right as I entered the central courtyard, I saw Hindou. She was standing in front of her mother's apartment.

We had never been as close as sisters should be, even though we were born the same year and enrolled in school together. In those first years of innocence, she had been my best friend. Then, as we grew older, we had championed the causes of our respective mothers in the quarrels they were constantly getting into.

But today we shared the same destiny. And Hindou had relaxed her defiance toward me. Tormented, she bared her face, darkened by large circles that betrayed sleepless nights. She gestured for me to follow her and led me outside into the large kitchen. Enormous pots of meat sauce simmered on the coals, a prelude to the upcoming morning feast. The area was still calm, for it was barely dawn. Hindou shivered despite the heat, rubbed her hands together and warmed them by the fire. Turning her back to me, she asked in a muffled voice:

"So? How are you feeling about getting married today? Are you afraid?"

"I'm sad. Why do you ask? Are you afraid?"

She turned back toward me and, to my great surprise, a torrent of tears sprang from her eyes. Preoccupied by my own fate, I hadn't given much thought to my sister's situation. I assumed she got along well with her fiancé, who was none other than the son of our uncle Moussa. I believed she was in love with him, and, in any event, it seemed to me that she was luckier than I was.

Moubarak was barely twenty-two years old and wasn't ugly. Quite the contrary!

"I'm afraid of him," she murmured.

"Afraid? But why?"

"Are you not aware of the problem he had before his father proposed we marry?"

Moubarak was a big drinker and didn't hide it. All you had to do was smell his foul breath. For some time now, he had stopped going out in the morning. He wasn't seen until afternoon or night. He shunned his father, who had refused to give him the capital to enter the shoe business in Douala. My uncle was skeptical about negotiations on the coast and had already given him money a few years prior when Moubarak had wanted to go into the timber trade like his uncle Yougouda. All of it had been spent on girls, clubs, and clothes. Even worse, not only had he become an alcoholic, he had started taking tramadol, a powerful painkiller ravaging the population of Maroua. All those rumors remained without consequence until the day when Moubarak, blackout drunk, sexually assaulted his mother's young maid. With no means of defense, the young woman was simply sent back to her village with a five-thousand-franc bill as her only compensation. As for Moubarak, his father decided it was high time for him to start a family. He didn't look far: Hindou was of marrying age and the family admired her tranquil and submissive nature. A perfect arrangement! Her calmness would channel Moubarak's excessive energy. The two fathers ratified their decisions without consulting those involved.

Hindou continued:

"One day, he dragged me into his bedroom and tried to kiss me!"

"What?" I exclaimed, scandalized. "What did you do?"

"I pushed him off, of course, but he grabbed me by the arm. So I bit him until I drew blood and managed to flee, but he promised to have his revenge on our wedding night. Oh my God, Ramla, I'm so afraid of him!"

"You didn't tell your mother what happened?"

"What am I supposed to say to her? It's not the kind of thing we discuss with our mothers, you know."

Hindou sobbed. I felt helpless in the face of such distress.

"Ramla, I wish I could marry Alhadji Issa instead of Moubarak. He's a lowlife. I'm afraid of him. You're lucky."

The house was already waking up. It was time for us to prepare for the most important day of our lives.

IX

When the guests were assembled, the imam entered, holding a plank inscribed with the final verses of the Quran. He had Hindou repeat the sacred text, then me. All the women around us were crying. Each one was reliving her own anguish and disappointments through us, something I would understand only years later. When the marabout's role was complete, a griot stood up and recited three times in a piercing voice:

"O illustrious ones! Aldhaji Issa, son of Alhadji Hamadou, is marrying Ramla, daughter of Alhadji Boubakari. The dowry is ten heads of oxen, already paid. We have all heard! Bear witness. May God bless this union!"

After a short prayer, my marriage was sealed.

Hindou's marriage followed the same ritual a few minutes later.

"O illustrious ones! Another *tégal*. Moubarak, son of Alhadji Moussa, is marrying Hindou, daughter of Alhadji Boubakari. The dowry is two hundred thousand francs, already paid. We have all heard! Bear witness. May God bless this union. And may He grant them all a blessed progeny and immense riches."

Then came the celebration, with dozens of horses, griots who sang our praises to the sound of drums, dances around a gigantic banquet. Excluded from all this revelry, the women listened from inside their apartments, trying to guess the dance steps or the song lyrics. In the bedroom, where Hindou and I spent the day awaiting our great departure, the young girls from school and the family were listening to the music and dancing. Hindou looked serene, which surprised me. She even smiled a little. From time to time, I met her gaze. She looked like a happy bride, and I admired her self-control. I, on the other hand, was stupefied. How was it possible? To be married to a fifty-year-old man, at seventeen? Me, the prettiest, most intelligent, most cheerful girl in all the town?

O my father! I don't understand. Your business is flourishing just like my uncle's, so why sacrifice me to such great greed? There are so many girls in the family, including several who would be happy to take my place, so why me?

O my father! You have so many children, but it's convenient to have girls. You can be rid of them so easily.

O my father! You say you know Islam like the back of your hand. You force us to be veiled, to say our prayers, to respect our traditions, so why do you deliberately ignore the precept of the Prophet which stipulates that a girl must consent to her marriage?

O my father! Your pride and your interests will always take precedence. Your wives and your children are mere pawns on the chessboard of your life, in the service of your personal ambitions.

O my father! Your respect of tradition takes priority over our wishes and our desires, no matter the suffering your decisions cause.

O my father, did you ever love us? Yes, you will say, and you are doing all of this for our own good. After all, us young girls, what do we know about life? How could we choose our husbands?

But if you deem us incapable, perhaps it's because we are not yet of the age to marry.

O my father! I understand, we live in a city hostile to change, where one must conform to tradition, but is that the only reason for your choice? Could you imagine for a single moment that you might be wrong?

O my father! I can't even be mad at you. I am a girl, to my dismay. I could never, like a boy, take refuge one day in your bosom or cry on your shoulder. That isn't done. A girl cannot approach her father, a girl cannot embrace her father.

His eyes betrayed no nostalgia, no regret. Despite my bitterness, I hoped to read some affection in them, now that the time to leave him had arrived. I wished I could shout my feelings.

And you, my mother! Out of concern for security or out of pride, you sacrificed me. You want to turn me into a rich woman. You want to see me behind the wheel of a car, you want me to be idolized and respected. You want to keep raising the bar for your co-wives, and you put that on me. You love me, you admire me. I am your daughter and I am perfect. No matter what I want, I must be perfect and envied.

O my mother! I am mad at you. You love me, of course! But you loved me badly. You could not understand me or defend me. You did not hear my cry of distress.

You threw me out to pasture. But you are still my mother. The person I love most in the world.

O my mother! I feel guilty for causing you pain. I've always tried to be the person you dreamed I would be. Never have I succeeded. You liked to compare Hindou's calm and my turbulence. You managed to instill me with complexes and dissatisfaction.

I had be the best, the most intelligent, the prettiest. I had to be your dream. Your daughter! Your hope! You always told me that I was the indirect cause of your suffering, but also of your joy. You stayed here for me. Now it's up to me to make sure you never regret it.

O my mother! It's difficult to be a girl, to always set a good example, always obey, always practice self-control, always be patient!

O my mother, I love you so much, but I'm mad at you today.

O my mother, get ahold of yourself! Look at me. Do I seem happy the way a bride should be?

And you, mother, are you happy as the mother of the bride? Why those tears? Why that outrageous makeup, you who never wear makeup? Why those red eyes behind the black kohl?

That night, my aunts prepared the water that would, according to custom, be used to bathe us. They added a few pinches of henna, perfume, and kola nuts. Then they dressed us in rich and sparkling pagnes, put some light makeup on us, and adorned us with gold jewels. They spritzed us with perfume and finally covered us in large black embroidered coats decorated with shining stones. Our faces were entirely covered by hoods.

I tried to meet my mother's gaze but it wasn't visible, and neither was Hindou's. Quickly, our aunts led us to our father's apartment, where we wouldn't leave except to enter the cars that awaited us.

Our respective mothers chose not to say goodbye to us. Was it to better hide their tears and distress?

X

The usual advice a father gives to his daughter when she gets married and, by ricochet, to all the women present, we already know by heart. It can be summed up in a single, unique recommendation: be submissive!

Accept everything your husband does. He is always correct; he has all the rights and we have all the duties. If the marriage succeeds, it will be because of our obedience, our good character, our willingness to compromise; if it fails, it will be our fault alone, the consequence of our bad behavior, our detestable character, our lack of restraint. In conclusion: patience, *munyal* faced with hardship, with sadness, with pain.

"*Alhamdulillah!*" says our father.

We know that a girl can drive her father to hell. They say that each step of a pubescent, unmarried girl is tallied in the great book and inscribed as a sin for her father. Each drop of impure blood from an unmarried adolescent hurries her father to hell.

"*Alhamdulillah!*"

We know that the worst sin for a father is his daughter having sex outside of marriage. A true believer will spare himself Allah's anger. His daughter will be married as soon as possible in order to avoid the worst torment a father can suffer.

"*Alhamdulillah!*"

My father will be spared. He married his daughters properly. He carried out a divine duty. To raise girls and bring them, still virgins, to their protectors chosen by God. He unburdened himself of a great responsibility.

Henceforth, his daughters will no longer belong to him.

"Alhamdulillah!"

My father can now rest easy. He has honorably fulfilled the difficult mission Allah entrusted to him in granting him daughters.

Distraught, I burst into sobs before my father's indifferent gaze. My aunt Nenné gestures to me and takes me outside. My in-laws, covered in gold and precious pagnes, stand near the luxurious cars and stamp their feet with impatience. My aunt drags me by the arm, readjusts the hood that covers my face, and puts me in a Mercedes. I glance at Hindou. My aunt Diya is pushing her into a flamboyant car, a convertible decorated with ribbons. Several mopeds are parked outside, meant to accompany us with as much noise as possible.

Throughout the trip, I cry. There are curious onlookers who, gathered at the side of the road, greet the nuptial procession with shouts. I want to scream at them:

"Save me, I beg you, they're stealing my happiness and my youth! They're separating me forever from the man I love. They're forcing me to live a life I don't want. Save me, I beseech you, I'm not happy like you think I am! Save me, before I become one of those shadows hidden inside a compound forevermore. Save me before I languish amid four walls, a captive. Save me, I beg you, they're snatching away my dreams, my hopes. They're stripping me of my life!"

HINDOU

At the end of patience,
there is the sky.

AFRICAN PROVERB

I

P atience, my girls! *Munyal!* Integrate it into your future life. Inscribe it in your heart, repeat it in your mind. *Munyal!* Such is the sole value of marriage and of life. Such is the true value of our religion, of our customs, of *pulaaku*. *Munyal*, you must never forget it. *Munyal*, my girls! For patience is a virtue."

"God loves those who are patient," my father says.

I didn't wait to get married to follow my father's advice. I had always understood this famous *munyal*. So much suffering! I wonder when I heard that word for the first time. Probably at my birth. They must have sung to me: "Patience, *munyal*, my baby! You have entered a world made of suffering. Little girl, so young and so impatient! You are a girl. So, *munyal* all your life. Starting right now! A woman's period of happiness is short. Patience, my girl, starting now . . ."

My hand seeks my sister Ramla's, grips it tightly, but the advice our father must provide to us before we leave has reached its end. My aunts are already leading us toward the exit.

At this final moment, I wished I could hide in my mother's bed. I wished I could cling to her until the end of my days. I wished I could grovel at my father's feet with no regard for that patience he was always harping on about, listening only to my terror, begging him to renounce this marriage. I would have given even my last breath to hear my father say: "You are too young. Moubarak will have to wait."

Too late! I am married. To Moubarak, this cousin I had often seen but never known. He lives a stone's throw away from us. He probably referred to me as his slave or his wife when I was little. I've always seen him around; he could've very well been my brother. I am married to Moubarak, and henceforth I belong to my uncle Moussa's compound.

In truth, I've always belonged to my uncle Moussa's compound. The strength of our family ties made each of my uncles a second father to me. Their houses were also mine, and not only could I go there as often as I liked, but I could even live there without having to ask my parents' permission. However, tonight, they led me to my uncle Moussa's not as a daughter, but as a daughter-in-law. O my father, why me? Did it cross your mind that I might not consent? And that I have the right not to consent? I don't love Moubarak. Worse—I detest him.

Before, when we were younger, I was completely indifferent to him. He was just one of my cousins, one among dozens of cousins. He was neither good nor bad, neither better nor worse. Until the day he started to drink and take drugs, and ended up crossing the Rubicon by sexually assaulting his mother's maid. From that point on, he became the worst of them all. And then came the day my mother informed me that I had been promised to him.

Uncle Moussa's compound is the very embodiment of chaotic polygamy. Since we were kids, we've heard all sorts of scandals. The co-wives, bitter rivals, whose quarrels play out through knife fights between brothers, girls repudiated and remarried, accusations of hiring marabouts, using sorcery, drugs, or alcohol. My uncle, authoritarian, lives in the middle of his compound with such arrogance and such distance that he is always the last to know what's going on within his family. As soon as he enters his house, there is an immediate silence. Even his wives seem not to have any intimacy with him. Each tries to protect her children the best she can. Despite his severity, Uncle Moussa has more and more difficulty earning the respect of his eldest sons. Those who skipped their studies can't seem to get their affairs in order and loiter all day with no hope for the future besides receiving an inheritance one day. The atmosphere in the compound is more and more tense. Uncle Moussa takes refuge increasingly in the mosque or at his store, where he has to be extremely vigilant because his children have a tendency to steal from him at every opportunity.

I started to hate Moubarak the day I ran into him while I was visiting my best friend, his sister, and he called out to me:

"Hey, Hindou, my future wife, are you here to visit your fiancé?"

"Of course not! What are you talking about?"

"Come here! Let's consummate the engagement since we can't consummate the marriage yet."

Moubarak then dragged me to his bedroom. I struggled to wriggle out of his grasp, but he kissed me shamelessly.

I bit him violently, nauseated by his foul stench. He reeked of alcohol. Taking advantage of his momentary distraction, I escaped. Enraged, he swore:

"You little brat! You bit me, but you just wait. You'll get what's coming to you."

Since that day, I've avoided him, and if I happened to run into him, he would greet me, smiling, and then, with a malicious wink, tell me that he couldn't wait to marry me. I became more and more uneasy, and over time, my sense of unease has turned to panic. I dread my marriage, especially the wedding night.

Ramla squeezes my hand, trying to transmit to me some of her strength and courage.

Already, my father concludes:

"May Allah grant you happiness and bless your home with many children and much *baraka*. Now go!"

Then I lose all my composure and fall to the floor in sobs. My father says nothing while my aunt Diya tries to lift me up and force me out the door.

Breaking my reserve, and to everyone's surprise, I cry out to my stupefied father:

"Please, Baaba, I don't want to marry Moubarak! Please, let me stay here."

"What are you saying, Hindou?"

"I don't love Moubarak. I don't want to marry him."

I sob even harder. My aunts hold their breath, shocked by my despair and by the scene I'm making in front of my father—I, who used to be cited as an example of calm and docility. They're afraid of their brother's reaction. But, defying all expectations, my father simply shakes his head and orders his sisters to leave.

Then I start to shout, to cry, and I stubbornly refuse to leave. In my terror to marry the man they're forcing on me, I have no more honor or dignity.

"Please, Father, please, I don't love Moubarak, I don't want to marry him."

I beg him, sobbing even harder and clinging to the sofa with all my might.

"Go," my father repeats, still calm. With great difficulty, Goggo Diya wrests me from my refuge and pushes me out the door while trying to comfort me. Every bride cries when she leaves the parental compound. I'm just more sensitive than others. There's no need to make a big deal out of it.

"Please, Baaba, I beg you, I don't want him. I'll take anyone but him . . ."

I continue to struggle and manage to escape my aunt's arms. I fall at my father's feet.

"Please, Father, for the love of Allah, do not force me to go!"

"That's enough of this childishness," my uncle says then with a sarcastic smile. "You are greatly disappointing me, Hindou. You who they called sensible. It's clear you understood none of the advice you've just been given. Go, Diya! I've had enough with the hysterics."

Still sobbing, I submit and the women thrust me out. Helped by a cousin, Goggo Diya pushes me firmly into the car, which takes off at full speed, as though in a hurry to split open the crowd. We hear horns and the youyous of girls heaped into other cars. Although the conjugal house is in a section of my uncle Moussa's compound and just a few feet from my father's, Moubarak wants to make sure his wedding doesn't go unnoticed. Sirens blaring, he throws himself at the front of the procession among the dozens of motorcycles and cars to make the tour of the town.

II

I didn't wait long! Even though tradition dictates the young groom be driven home by his friends late at night when the rest of the house is asleep, and that he be as discreet as possible, Moubarak soon enters the bedroom, leaving the others to celebrate in front of the courtyard, seated on rugs, sipping tea and coffee, chatting noisily. The women who accompanied me are asleep in my apartment, constructed at the same time as Moubarak's, across the compound. The smell of fresh paint permeates the rooms, only slightly masking the stench of cow dung; before Uncle Moussa decided to construct four apartments for the two marriages, mine included, this land was a stockyard. They simply poured in sand from the neighboring stream to disperse the odor and get the space ready for construction. As soon as he enters the bedroom, without even looking at me, Moubarak puts on music. Sitting on the rug, in the darkest corner, I curl up as much as possible. I feel my throat choked with anxiety.

"There she is! My cousin and dear wife! Come here. Let's consummate the marriage quickly. I told you this day would soon arrive."

"Please . . ."

"Stop with the foolishness and take off your clothes—now! I hate prudish women."

Racked with anxiety, I know something isn't right. Moubarak hasn't just been drinking. He's also taken tramadol pills cut with Viagra. A typical cocktail for him, and for other young men around here. You can find those pills on every street corner, at the neighborhood grocer and every street vendor. The night of the honeymoon, men take drugs to reinvigorate themselves, to guarantee a certain endurance and virility to match their spirited ardor.

"Take off your clothes. You look ridiculous in those veils."

"I beg you . . ."

"You want to play? Okay, we'll play. It's even better when you resist a little. It'll be fun to strip you."

He turns up the music, then calmly starts to undress himself. I retreat even more into the corner. I'm so afraid that my teeth chatter and I tremble like a leaf. He sits on the bed, glances at me unkindly, and says:

"So? Are you coming on your own or would you rather I come and get you?"

"Please . . ."

He stands up brusquely and, catching me off guard, throws me onto the bed and tears off my clothes. I defend myself as best I can. When he rips off my corsage, I bite him ferociously. He withdraws his hand where beads of blood are now forming. Furious, he starts to hit me. I scream, I fight back, a violent strike knocks me out and I fall onto the bed.

A few hours later, I have no more strength to scream nor tears to cry. Silence reigns in the bedroom. I've screamed, cried, and begged so much that I have no more voice. I gather myself on the bed, my wounded body covered in bruises. I'm bleeding enough to soak the bed. I'm in a lot of pain. I try to stand up.

Moubarak, sleeping next to me, wakes immediately and looks at me with contempt.

"Did you sleep well, dear cousin? Hey, what am I saying—dear *wife*! Don't move, I'll be right there."

"No, please!"

"Are you starting up your claptrap again?"

"Sorry, I'm hurt. I'm in pain."

"Don't worry! That's normal."

He looks at the bed with disgust and drags me to the ground. I fall roughly and start to scream. He gags me with his hand.

"It's very early. Everyone is still sleeping. Be quiet! You made enough noise last night. I never would have thought you could be such a scaredy-cat. They'll think I killed you! This time, you shut your mouth!"

He rapes me again. The pain is so sharp that I slip into a merciful unconsciousness.

No one was scandalized by my state. It wasn't a crime! Moubarak had every right to do with me what he wanted, and all he had done was fulfill his conjugal duties. Admittedly, he had been a bit brutal, but he was a virile young man in good health. On top of it, I was so beautiful! Of course, he lost his mind around so much charm. He was just so in love! I also deserved congratulations, for I had kept myself pure. I had not dishonored my family.

It's not a crime! It's a legitimate act! The conjugal duty. It's not a sin. Quite the contrary. Whether for me or Moubarak, it's a blessing granted by Allah.

It's not rape. It's proof of love. Nevertheless, they advise Moubarak to restrain his ardor given the stitches my wound required. They consoled me. This is marriage. Next time, it'll be better. Also, this is patience, the very *munyal* they told you about. A woman experiences several painful stages in her life. What happened is simply a part of that. All I had to do was eat porridge spiced up with natron and take some warm baths to speed up my healing process.

The conjugal duty! They cited me a hadith of the Prophet: Unhappy is the woman who angers her husband, and happy is the woman whose spouse is pleased with her! I would be better off learning to satisfy my husband.

The doctor wasn't shocked either. It wasn't rape. Everything had unfolded normally. I was simply a new bride who's more sensitive than others. My husband is young and in love! Of course he's passionate! It's normal for things to happen this way. For that matter, who would dare utter the word "rape"? Rape doesn't exist in marriage.

Goggo Diya told me later that she'd been ashamed of me for screaming so much. Everyone must have heard me. I had continued to shout at the hospital while they gave me stitches. I had been indecent. She had been so embarrassed on my wedding night that she had almost left. Even my father and stepfather must have known that my husband was touching me! Such shame! Such immodesty! Such vulgarity! That moment was supposed to be secret. How would I meet their gazes now? Such a lack of courage, of *munyal*! Such a lack of *semteende*, of restraint! Where was the *pulaaku* they had inculcated in me? The Fulani die like lambs, quietly, not bleating like goats. It was my fault I had suffered more than others. If I had given in, I wouldn't have had to endure all that! In fact, Goggo Nenné had told her that Ramla had been just as pure as me, but no one had heard a peep from her on her wedding night.

I went quiet. I had nothing left to say.

My aunts hurriedly cooked the *bassissé*, a porridge made of rice, milk, and butter. They distribute it to all the family, and especially to the young girls to show them that I, Hindou, had remained a virgin until marriage. A way of encouraging them to do the same.

Thus, they cared for my body, but not my soul. No one thought about the deeper and more painful wounds inside me. They repeated that nothing dramatic had happened. Just something banal. Nothing more than a traumatizing wedding night. And aren't all wedding nights traumatizing? They told me I had understood none of my father's advice.

> *I owe my husband submission!*
> *I must keep my mind from distraction!*
> *I must be his slave so that he will be my captive!*
> *I must be his earth so that he will be my sky!*
> *I must be his field so that he will be my rain!*
> *I must be his bed so that he will be my hut!*

The day after the wedding, everyone went back to their houses while I settled into my new life. Moubarak curtailed his passions a bit, but he didn't utter a word of regret. Nothing had happened. We were married, weren't we?

III

The days and nights went by, and all looked alike in the monotony of my uncle's large compound. I adhered to the familial habits, immutable since the dawn of time.

My uncle was now my father-in-law. I had to carefully avoid him, take off my shoes before walking near him, lower my eyes and bend my knee to greet him. And I had to keep my veil on my head in the presence of my aunt, who was now my mother-in-law. I could neither eat nor drink in front of her. I also had to avoid speaking, gossiping, or laughing in front of her. My cousin Moubarak had become my husband. I owed him submission and respect.

I got up early at the rooster's crow for the first daily prayer. The whole house woke up at the same time and each person had a strictly defined task. The women, when they weren't yoked to the kitchen chores, cleaned their apartments. Young maids would sweep the common spaces. The children, regardless of their education, began their days reading the Quran under the surveillance of a master marabout—except for Thursday and Friday, the Islamic weekend.

Uncle Moussa personally assured that everyone was awake at dawn and didn't hesitate to knock on the doors of the stubborn. *Fortune to those who wake up early, failure to respect this truth will bring misfortune, or even a terrible calamity!* he would rant.

For the cooking, we—my uncle's four wives, my cousins' wives, and me—took turns. The *defande*, the kitchen shift, lasted twenty-four hours: it started with the nightly meal and ended after lunch the next day. Our mothers-in-law let us prepare the meals while they took charge of the distribution for each familial group. Above all, they had to make sure our lack of experience didn't lead us to incorrect distribution. The most important dish, cooked for the men, was served in the *zawleru*, then the meal for the women, finally the meal for the children by sex and age. Each daughter-in-law also had to help her mother-in-law when it was her turn. Typically, she would end up taking over all the domestic chores.

The menu lacked originality, it wasn't healthy, and it didn't change—or only very slightly. Uncle Moussa slaughtered lambs, chickens, or an ox. The essential parts were saved in the freezer, while the other parts were fried or dried. We ate meat for each meal. With tomato sauce, braised, boiled, or with vegetables. Rice was the most commonly consumed grain, sometimes replaced by red millet, sorghum, or corn. We usually started the day with rice in meat sauce, drinking either fresh cow's milk or porridge with curdled milk and peanut paste. There was also coffee or tea prepared each morning, which we saved for the rest of the day in large thermoses. Only the men could have doughnuts or bread, for if these foods had been open to all the house, with more than twenty adults and dozens of children, it would have cost a fortune, which my uncle did not deem appropriate.

We didn't have the right to serve ourselves alone. It was the *daada-saaré*, my uncle's first wife, who was in charge of giving us what we had to prepare, taking into account the impromptu visits of distant family members or acquaintances. When she was absent or unavailable, it was the second wife who was responsible for the compound.

At night, the men dined separately. A cook, hired by my uncle, prepared a meal specially for them, more varied and richer than that of the women. Along with the indispensable bowl of couscous in vegetable sauce, they generally ate plantain or potato fries, meat of course but also braised fish, porridge, salad, and tea or coffee.

During this time, us women also ate together. It wasn't possible for one of us to dine alone, and we certainly couldn't have a special plate. If I had a particular desire, I would call for my mother, who would discreetly bring me the dish in question, or else I would ask Moubarak—the days he was in a good mood, of course!

We spent a lot of time together, us women, working in the large *hangar* in front of the apartments of our mothers-in-law, which then served as a common area for all the women of the house. That's where we chatted, shelled peanuts, cut vegetables, braided, or drew henna tattoos for hours on our hands and feet. We could also watch television, but only Arabic channels. Because one day, when he had caught his wives absorbed in a series in which kissing took up the majority of the plot, Uncle Moussa had forbidden Western and African channels. Wild with rage, he had immediately called a technician to block what he called the "devil's channels." The man had left us access to Bollywood films, whose romantic love stories enchanted us when the master of the house was absent. As soon as he came back, the only thing we watched was the Mecca channel—the voice of imams.

Moubarak watched whatever he desired. He had cable and accessed all the available Western channels. He also had a DVD player and procured X-rated films. It was his latest accessory that he used to torment me. He forced me to reenact the scenes he watched. It was an opportunity to insult me, to hurt me by relating his multiple dalliances that he defied me to tell the rest of the family, knowing I couldn't do so since, according to tradition, one never speaks of sex or of anything related to it. Over time, I found Moubarak to be an unpredictable man who could possess boundless aggression, but who could also be hypersensitive.

I sensed in him numerous wounds and an endless frustration, which he masked with a great scorn for propriety. But sometimes he would be in a relatively good mood. Then he could be charming and life by his side was bearable. Those days, he was especially thoughtful toward me, he spoke to me kindly, and we'd talk for hours. He would invite me to go out at night unbeknownst to my other family members, and we would take long walks and visit his friends. Sometimes he would tell me about his business dealings and confide his disappointment in his father, who refused to help finance his endeavors. I surprised myself by feeling sympathy for him in those moments.

But on his worst days, Moubarak could be in a horrendous mood. He sulked, barely speaking to me or getting angry at me for the smallest reason. On those days, I tried to be as discreet as possible. Fortunately, he would spend a lot of time in his bedroom taking pills, and only go out after nightfall. When he came back late, he would be blackout drunk. Even though we each had a room, I had to join him at night to share his bed. But on those drunken nights, I would lock myself in my bedroom and forgo that conjugal service for fear of suffering his abuse.

But one night, he came back around two in the morning and

pounded on my door. I ignored him, pretending to be in a deep sleep. He knocked louder.

"Hindou, open up! You're not allowed to sleep outside the conjugal bedroom. Open the door or I'll break it down, and then you'll be sorry . . ."

He made so much noise that I was afraid he would wake up the whole house. I was even more afraid that he'd fulfill his threat. I dressed immediately. I had barely opened the door when I received a fist to my right eye.

"That's to teach you respect. You have no right to lock the door. You wait for me, no matter what time I get home. Is that clear?"

I swayed and, trying to balance, grabbed the curtains, whose supports fell to the floor with a loud crash. Hamza, one of Moubarak's younger brothers, hurried to the bedroom just in time to stop Moubarak from delivering his second strike.

"Moubarak, what's gotten into you? She hasn't done anything! Look at what time you're waking up your wife to hit her!"

"Mind your own business. She's my wife and I'll do with her what I like."

"Yes, she's your wife. That's exactly why you shouldn't hit her. At least show a bit of consideration for your cousin, or for your uncle, her father. If one of you should be angry, it's her. You've just come home at two in the morning!"

"Just because you're afraid of your wife doesn't mean I have to fear mine. Look at you, little Hamza, always so obedient, a good little boy. Your wife has no respect for you. You're like her little dog. You bring shame to all men!"

He didn't take it any further. Hamza stopped him with a punch. Madina, Hamza's wife, got involved. The two of us tried to separate the two brothers. In vain. Soon it was the mothers' turn to intervene, then the other brothers. Finally, Uncle Moussa himself was the one to put an end to the general tumult.

Hamza was reproached for his lack of respect for his elder brother. Decorum dictates that the eldest is always right. However, everyone knew Hamza was trying to defend me, which showed respect for my father, his uncle, and was therefore honorable. Even so, he could have found an alternative!

I was reproached for going to sleep before my husband's return. For that matter, what was I doing in my apartment at night? As far as they knew, I had no co-wife, Hamza's mother scolded me. It is custom that I be in my apartment only during the day. A wife is supposed to share a bed with her husband. I had asked for it!

My mother-in-law reproached me privately for my impoliteness and my disobedience toward my husband. She reminded me of my duties as a wife, encouraged me to be more docile, and threatened to shun me. My behavior had threatened the fragile equilibrium between two brothers who couldn't stand each other and who had no need for another excuse to kill each other. On top of that, she was also now at risk of arguing even more with the most foul-tempered of her co-wives, Hamza's mother.

I acquiesced to everything.

In the following days, Moubarak ignored me. He, and the rest of my family, avoided meeting the gaze of my black eye. It was nothing but a misunderstanding. Yet another one.

IV

I t's a scorching afternoon, common in March, in Maroua. The
sky is a deep blue. The heat is suffocating. Forty-five degrees.
In this torpor, the compound is silent. Even the children have
stopped playing. We all seek refuge in the shade. Seated on my veranda, I knit a new floral blanket. While my fingers work around
the silk thread, I let my mind run free, lost in thought.

Suddenly, the roar of a motorcycle makes me lift my head.
Moubarak arrives, accompanied by a young girl with a brazen
air, dressed in a form-fitting dimity dress showing off her curves.
Around twenty years old, she's perched on her stiletto heels, which
on the sandy ground risk spraining her ankles. Moubarak looks at
me defiantly, then brings his guest into the living room.

I can hear their lively conversation, punctuated with bursts of
laughter that lance my heart like needles. What should I do? I
don't want to cause a scandal. Parents and relatives would certainly reproach me for disgracing Moubarak, for not preserving
the dignity and honor of my husband. While I reflect on the best
course of action, standing on the veranda, indignant and humiliated, I hear Moubarak close the door to his apartment. The click
of the key in the lock slices through me and wakes me from my
torpor. The purr of the air-conditioning in the conjugal bedroom
breaks the silence. My pride is so wounded that, trembling with

anger, I rush to my bedroom, put on my veil, and leave through the back door.

I've only been married for a few months and I don't yet have the right to go to my father's house, but I feel a profound desire to see my mother and confide in her. The street is deserted because of the heat wave.

At this hour, my stepmothers have likely retired to their apartments. I lower my veil and silently slip into my mother's bedroom just as she's finishing her prayer. She's still seated on the rug telling her beads. When she sees me, stupefied, before asking me anything, she rapidly glances outside, terrified. Relieved not to see any of her co-wives, she rushes to close her bedroom door.

"Hindou, what's going on? What are you doing here?"

I cry in silence. It's good to see her again. She, too, starts to cry. Then she squeezes me in her arms, emotional, worried. What horrible event could have forced a young newlywed to go out during the day? Worse, to go back to her parents' compound?

"Hindou," she repeats, "what's going on, my girl? Tell me quickly!"

"Moubarak!" I say, hiccuping. "Of course, I know he drinks, that he takes drugs, goes to the club, and has girlfriends . . ."

"Yes, everyone knows it. Your father knew it, too," she adds bitterly.

"He's with a girl in his bedroom, in our house, right now."

"What?" she asks, bewildered.

Her indignation is so great that her eyes gleam with a simmering rage. This time, Moubarak has crossed a line. Stunned, she starts to pace and then drops onto her bed.

"Maybe you misunderstood! It must be a friend of . . ."

I interrupt her and add, sitting at her side:

"They're locked inside."

"Impossible!"

My mother is my father's fourth wife—and the only educated one. She and her co-wives live in a permanent climate of conflict and jealousy; she doesn't want my misadventures to reach the family. My stepmothers will show solidarity on the surface but will have a good laugh in private, damaging my mother's pride and honor. We have to keep the co-wives from finding out, at least for now. They'll be only too happy to hear of the problems of the newest and preferred wife. Even though the co-wives pretend to get along, a tacit rivalry exists between them, which is played out through their children. It's not enough to detest their co-wife, they must hate all her children, too. They don't wish only for her misfortune, but for that of all her family. Above all, the father must not give special attention to any one of them.

My mother asks me to stay in her bedroom and immediately runs to see my father. It's not her *defande*. So she waits patiently for the third wife to leave his apartment to refill the water boiler for my father's ablutions.

"Doudou, I have to see Alhadji right away!"

"What's going on?" asks Doudou, shocked.

Except in cases of emergency, a wife must wait her turn to see her husband. Masking her irritation, Doudou insists:

"Is there a problem?"

"Nothing major. Not to worry. I just need to tell him something before he goes to the market. It's urgent!"

"Perhaps I can serve as an intermediary. He seems to be in a hurry. Just tell me what's going on and I'll talk to him."

"It's personal. Ask him to see me," my mother demands.

"I'll try!" Doudou says despite herself, barely concealing her curiosity and frustration.

My mother follows her and waits on the veranda. Glacial, my father ends up letting her in. He's just managed his books and set aside the portion destined for alms, the *zakat*, the third pillar of Islam. Though he doesn't hide his preference for my mother, he is still wary of her impertinence and her convictions, always unequivocal when something doesn't suit her. Since her daughter's wedding, she's been extremely cold to him, and he's starting to grow irritated by it. His wife refuses to understand that there are situations beyond him. Despite the great love he has for her, he couldn't disappoint his brother when he asked for his own daughter's hand for his son. Besides, what did she want? Since a daughter must be married, he had simply accomplished his duty as a father.

"So, Amraou, what brings you here? What is so pressing that you couldn't wait for your *defande*, which in fact begins tonight? If one of your co-wives had tried to see me during your turn, you would have made quite a scene."

"I had to speak to you right away. There's a problem!"

"Well, that I had guessed. Tell me quickly! I don't have time to waste. They're waiting for me."

"Hindou is here. She came back!"

"What? In the middle of the day? Before even a year of marriage has passed! What am I saying, before six months! She really is your daughter! No patience."

"You don't know what Moubarak did. He . . ."

68

"It doesn't matter what he did," he cuts her off with a gesture of his hand. "She could have at least waited for nightfall. To return to her parents' home sulking in the middle of the day when we live in the same neighborhood, when it's only been a few months since she's been married, it's ridiculous! You can go," he concludes, and dismisses my mother.

"But . . ."

"I said I understood. Go on," he grumbles. "Call my sister Nenné. And take her back discreetly. She's lucky I'm in too much of a rush to see her or else I'd teach her good manners. All this is your fault. You coddle your children too much, you spoil them. Of course they don't know how to behave. If you weren't so soft, she wouldn't have acted this way. It's because she knows that you'll support her that she came back. Do you think Ramla would dare do such a thing? I won't be going to see Hindou. Tell her to stay out of my way. She has no restraint!"

"Moubarak . . ."

"Have Nenné bring her back immediately and don't let anyone else find out. She really is your daughter! She never thinks about the consequences of her actions! What shame!"

"But her husband really took it too far. He . . ."

"It doesn't matter! It doesn't matter what Moubarak did, he's her cousin in addition to being her husband. The son of my brother. A bit of respect at least for her uncle. It's in difficult moments that one must be patient and bear everything. At most, if it's serious, she could have sent for her aunt to confide in her. But to come back like this! And you? What kind of mother are you? Instead of reprimanding her and sending her back discreetly, you come to bother me, interrupt my routine and pick a fight with your co-wife by forcing your way into my room before your turn. You're not much better than your daughter. Go and call Doudou for me!"

I cried all the tears I had in me upon learning what my father said. My mother, sitting in a corner of the bedroom, had a serious look on her face and her fists were clenched in anger. But, more than my father's decision, it was his disdainful attitude and hurtful words that enraged her. She understood his decision even though she didn't share his opinion. To console me, she told me her own story for the first time. Of course, I'd already heard it in bits and pieces but never from her mouth. Her eyes riveted to an invisible object, she gathered her memories. She wept silent tears, which she wiped occasionally with the end of her pagne. She was sad.

"You know, Hindou, I didn't choose to marry your father, but I also didn't refuse to do it. Why would I have said no? I never would have thought to refuse. Faced with the ordeal my family was going through at that time, I didn't have the heart to contradict my parents.

"My older sister had just died. A sudden and natural death that surprised the whole family. Resignation faced with the all-powerful desire of Allah replaced stupor and desolation. One does not die unless their time on earth has finished. A time already inscribed by the Creator from our first breath of life. We can neither speed up nor slow down the fateful moment. So why lament Allah's implacable decision? I hadn't thought about marriage. At least not at that point. I was fourteen and my older sister, married for a few years already to your father, had just died, leaving three orphans behind. In the family, we murmured that her death had been caused by a curse cast by a jealous co-wife. It was obvious:

my sister Hidaya was extremely beautiful, incredibly generous, and had rapidly become her husband's favorite.

"When she died, my mother, eyes red from sadness, summoned me to her bedroom. My father was there, his face dark. The two of them were praying in silence, counting their beads with one hand in a sign of resignation faced with the tragedy fate had imposed on them. I sat not far from my father, curious and impatient to know what they expected of me.

"'Amraou, your sister was a good daughter,' my father began after clearing his throat. 'In every respect. She will go to Paradise, *insh'Allah*. Her mother forgave her, her husband had nothing to reproach her for.'

"'Of course, Baaba!' I answered.

"'I also had nothing to reproach her for. She was always a kind and well-behaved daughter. She honored me and preserved my dignity.'

"'May Allah pardon her and welcome her,' my mother added in a murmur.

"'*Amine!*' my father responded. 'I've thought about it a great deal. For the last few days, I haven't been able to stop turning the same idea over in my head. I've just spoken to your mother about it and she has no objection. Quite the contrary! She agrees with me. Alhadji Boubakari was an irreproachable son-in-law, and it's a great loss for us. For him, too, since before becoming my son-in-law, he was my friend. What am I saying? My brother. We were circumcised together and went through the same hardships. Between us there is a great friendship, but also a great respect.'

"He paused, as though allowing his memories to flood back, then continued:

"'Amraou, you too are a well-behaved and obedient daughter. You have always known how to conduct yourself, and I know that I can trust you. You are already of marrying age. Thus, you will take your sister's place! You will raise her children and protect them as she would have done. You will live in her bedroom and inherit her belongings. You will marry Alhadji Boubakari one week from today. There will, of course, be neither a party nor any other celebration. I'm sorry we can't wait for summer vacation. But you are intelligent and have learned all you can at school. You know how to read and write. That's more than sufficient. The place of a woman is in her home. There you have it! I hope you'll be able to bring us honor and replace your sister.'

"In a stupor, I said nothing. What could I say? Everyone knows marriage is the only option for a girl. It was out of the question to contradict my parents. As the Fulani proverb says: 'What an elderly person sees sitting down, a child, even standing up, will not be able to see.'

"My father had chosen a husband for me. A man he valued and respected. As a worthy daughter, I had to obey his wishes. I had one week to get used to the idea. I knew my sister's house well. I had met her co-wives and played with their children. I had spent several nights in her bedroom and greeted her husband with respect each time I saw him. What an irony of fate to have to return, this time as a wife!

"'You will follow in her footsteps and you will replace her as mother to her children. May they never miss their mother,' my mother said. 'And when you have your own children, may your sister's children never feel wronged.'

"'I have already informed Boubakari of my decision,' my father added. 'He was very moved. I'm happy with this arrangement that satisfies everyone in the painful times we're going through. Allah watches over suffering souls. Here's some happiness in the wake of great misfortune!'

"Tears ran down my cheeks. My mother was also silently weeping. My father stood up and simply said:

"'Patience, *munyal!* We cannot go against God's will.'

"That's how I entered life as a married woman. No fanfare. They simply moved me into my sister's bedroom. They gave me everything that had belonged to her. Then, at nightfall, they brought me to my husband's bedroom. I didn't have time to learn to be a wife or mother. But those are things that aren't taught. A woman is born a wife and mother before all else. Yes, your older brothers are your half brothers, and they are also your cousins. No, they are simply your brothers, for I loved them, protected them, and raised them as my own. I inherited three of Hidaya's children, I also inherited the plates in her cabinet, furniture given to her by our father as a wedding gift, I even inherited her husband, but mostly I inherited her three co-wives! Patience! They repeated that to me often. Our rivalries as co-wives are not only endless, but a truce is impossible, for each rival impatiently awaits an opportunity to destabilize her enemy. I learned to protect myself from everything. The co-wives are the known enemies, but the sly stepsisters, the jealous wives of the stepbrothers, the husband's children, his mother, his family, are all enemies, too."

For a little while now, the tears streaming down my mother's cheeks had broken up her voice. And in a barely stifled sob, she concluded:

"A woman's life path is difficult, my girl. Our carefree moments are brief. We have no youth. We experience very little joy. We find happiness only where we cultivate it. It's up to you to find a solution to render your life bearable. Better yet, to render your life acceptable. That's what I did for all those years. I trampled on my dreams to better embrace my duties."

My aunt Nenné, whom my mother had called, entered the bedroom without knocking. Goggo Nenné was my mother's friend, they got along very well, and my mother hoped that her sister-in-law would have good advice in this humiliating situation. To see her daughter unhappy and devalued broke her heart. But the worst was for her to know that the misfortunate would delight her co-wives, who would be thrilled to add to it, thus tarnishing the image she had worked hard to cultivate as the favorite wife.

As soon as she walked through the door, Goggo Nenné exclaimed, her big eyes full of shock, her hand over her mouth:

"Hindou? What are you doing here? What is she doing here? Did something bad happen?" she asked, turning toward my mother.

"That loser husband of hers . . . What a curse, my God! Her father has asked that you take her back discreetly. No one knows she's here. No one can know, especially not those co-wife witches of mine!"

"You're right! Get up, Hindou! We'll go right away before anyone sees you. Frankly, my girl, you've gone too far. No matter the situation, you should at least wait for nightfall before going out. Shameful! Think about the consequences of your actions!"

"Moubarak is with another girl in our bedroom!" I confided, indignant and powerless.

"Ya Allah! No *pulaaku*, that boy! To do that to your wife! Worse, to your cousin! What shame, my God! What is happening to the world?"

"He has no scruples. If only Alhadji had listened to me! He would never have agreed to this marriage. I want to skin that boy alive!"

"We don't solve this kind of problem with violence, Amraou. I told you not to stand idly by, but you persist in ignoring things. Continue like this and not only will your enemies take care of it, they'll leave none of your children in peace! If you had consulted the marabouts as I told you to, if you had protected your daughter, if you had made a bit of effort for her husband to like her, this wouldn't have happened. You are naive, Amraou. And your daughter is even more so than you! You've just delighted your mother's enemies, Hindou. All those who hate her will only rejoice in your misfortune. You opened your milk gourd and let the flies lap it up!"

"What should we do, Nenné?" my mother asked. "I haven't been asleep as you imply. I have defended myself as best I could but too many people are set against me. What can I do alone against all of them? Where can I find this famous protection? Do you know someone good?"

"I've heard people talk about a great marabout in a neighboring village."

"Can you look into it?"

"I'll do it tomorrow, *insh'Allah*. In the meantime, Hindou, get up; I'll take you back. Be discreet, ignore Moubarak. A wife has no need to leave her home. Even there, you can find ways to show your husband you're angry. You also need to understand that when you recount certain things, it's not him you humiliate, it's yourself. And get it into your head once and for all that your actions reflect back on your mother."

Moubarak has relations with his mistress in the conjugal bedroom before my eyes. But I'm the one at fault. I'm the one who has no patience!

Moubarak brought his mistress back to the conjugal home, and it's the fault of my stepmothers, who must have cast a spell on me. It's the fault of my mother-in-law, who detests me, it's the fault of that girl who charmed him, it's the fault of my mother, who couldn't protect herself or me.

Tomorrow, Goggo Nenné will take care of it. . . .

V

Herbs to make me invincible, *gaadé* to procure me the charm I seem to be lacking, powders to put in Moubarak's tea without him knowing in order to guarantee his attachment to me, and many other miraculous products: that's what Goggo Nenné brought back from the marabout.

But nothing seems to work! Nothing breaks Moubarak's bad habits. Neither the herbs nor the prayers nor my submission, not even my patience. My husband has multiple dalliances, he drinks, takes drugs, and always comes home late. He continues to abuse me, to barrage me with insults as degrading as they are humiliating. His strikes leave me with countless bruises, scratches, scars—to my family members' total indifference. They know Moubarak hits me, but that's the way things go. It's natural for a man to correct, insult, or repudiate his wives. Neither my father nor my uncles are exceptions to that rule. All of them, one day or another, had to hit their wives. They don't think twice about hurting women, children, and employees. Why would my case be any different? Why should it be cause for concern? *It's a divine right,* an educated woman whispers to me one day. *It is written in the Quran that a man has the right to punish and strike his wife if she's disobedient. But it is still forbidden for him to go after her face.* She was scandalized by my black eye.

Barely older than a teenager and already I'm shrinking. It's as though unconsciously I were trying to disappear underground and make myself invisible. Pale, I drag around my meager skeleton. Floating in my pagnes, I can't stop walking, prey to anxiety. An insomniac, I spend my nights lying in the dark, spiraling through all sorts of morbid thoughts, and it's only in the early morning that I find a bit of respite, at the moment of the dawn prayer. I no longer live as I did at the beginning, following the immutable rhythm of the large compound, but rather according to Moubarak's changing moods, and the no less volatile moods of my mother-in-law and the rest of the women in the compound. In fact, the women are on top of one another all day to the point of feeling just as trapped by the high walls around us as by the dark and heavy fabrics my uncle Moussa forces us to wear. There's not a day when the women aren't up in arms or tearing one another apart after spinning in circles like lionesses in a cage.

Such boredom! Life goes by, and every day is the same. We have nothing to do but cook and take care of the children. Monotony consumes us, kills us from morning to night, night to morning.

As for Moubarak, he lives according to the rhythm of his breakdowns. He has no work, no hope for the future. His father refuses to give him even a franc for his business projects and calls him incapable, lazy, or a lowlife beyond repair. Idle, Moubarak deems no task suitable for him, above all does not want to work for anyone else, wants to take action but has lost all hope of help from any of his uncles because he's an alcoholic.

And so I have become his thing. He unleashes his excessive anger and bitterness toward his father onto me.

I've stopped complaining. When I cry, I do it secretly, at night, in the privacy of my bedroom. I no longer expect anything from others. Neither help nor hope. Resigned, I conform to what they all expect of me. I have no one to confide in. Between the women of the compound reigns the unsaid, hypocrisy, and mistrust.

I'm no exception: I'm becoming selfish. I'm not doing well, neither are the others, but I worry only about myself. My insomnia is getting worse, and the lack of sleep gives me migraines. I've taken medicine prescribed by doctors, potions recommended by healers, nothing works. Fatigue eats away at me; I feel an anguish that nothing can ease. I experience more and more numbness and cramps in my limbs, which leaves me depleted. Those around me say it's a cold, tell me to cover up and stay in bed. I sink gradually into depression and sometimes hyperventilate; my throat gets tight and I feel like I'm suffocating. My stomach in knots—death seems to me like the only escape.

One night when Moubarak comes back as usual, drunk and snarling, he demands that I make him a porridge. It's after midnight. I get to work, worried that at such a late hour I won't be able to find the right ingredients. In my fear, I can't manage to light the fire. Time passes, I grow desperate to satisfy my husband.

Tired of waiting, he joins me in the kitchen. And when he sees that the fire is still not lit, he becomes enraged. A sneer disfigures his face. Our gazes meet for a moment and then, saying nothing, he goes into the courtyard. I'm searching feverishly for a log when a violent blow to my back pushes me into the cinders. Stunned, I manage, through survival instinct, to turn around and protect my face as three more strikes with a parasol, as well as with numerous kicks, violently rain down on me.

"Make me my porridge right now or I'll come back to finish you off!" he threatens, turning back toward his bedroom.

My face swollen and my body full of bruises, I tremble throughout my limbs. My pagne is soiled with urine. I have to light the fire; I have to make the porridge. My hands shake so much that I spill a portion of the flour on the ground, and now I certainly won't have enough.

Moubarak returns quickly. His athletic silhouette surges from the darkness, his terrifying shadow moves through the doorway. In the silence, barely disturbed by my breath, I feel my heart racing and I start to beg, my teeth chattering:

"Please, I'm going as fast as I can! Please . . ."

As I retreat to the wall blackened with soot, I overturn the plate holding the rest of the flour and protect my face, repeating in a broken voice:

"I'm hurrying, it'll be ready soon! Give me a little more time, I'm almost done . . ."

"That's enough, Hindou! Forget the porridge. I don't want it anymore."

"I'll light the fire. I'll . . ."

Terror squeezes my throat, chokes me and stops me from breathing.

"I'll be done soon! I'll hurry."

When he approaches me, I'm trembling so much that, for the second time that night, I pee on myself. The warm liquid wets the already damp pagne, drips down my legs, and leaves a stain on the dusty floor. A void settles in my mind. My entire body contracts out of fear of more strikes. I'm terrified.

Unexpectedly, my fright calms him. He sighs.

I repeat, still retreating as if to blend into the wall:

"I'll make the porridge. I'll make it fast."

"Come," he says, taking me by the hand and leading me into the bedroom.

He seems to soften:

"Hindou, go take a shower, I'll wait for you," he orders me, closing the door.

"I'll make the porridge," I say, overwhelmed with fear.

"Go take a shower," he repeats.

Then, seeing that I'm still shaking, he pushes me into the bathroom and adds:

"It's over. I won't hit you again. Go wash up."

I take a shower, letting the water run over my wounded body as though to wash away my suffering. I try to stifle my sobs for fear of inciting his anger again, but I can't help myself. Eventually he leads me out of the bathroom, shaking.

Once I'm lying down next to him, Moubarak rapes me by way of consolation, repeating to me that it's my fault he hits me, that I always manage to make his blood boil. He advises me to be more conscientious from now on, and adds that he forgives me. Yawning, Moubarak concludes:

"Forget about it. I can see that I really scared you. I won't hit you again. It's just that I'm aggravated tonight. It's over! Sleep, my sweetheart! I love you, no matter what you might think."

I can't manage to close my eye. Next to me, his arms distractedly draped over my body, my husband sleeps a peaceful slumber. My back and neck, throbbing from the blows, ache more and more. If I stay there looking at him, enduring him without doing anything, Moubarak will end up killing me. His tenderness after a violent outburst is now a familiar scenario; it doesn't trick me anymore. It will always be the same. He'll hit me, pretend to regret it, promise to stop doing it . . . until the next time. I know this now.

Moubarak will not change. I could complain but they'll just tell me to be patient. A little longer. *He who has patience does not regret it*, they'll remind me. If a bad strike finishes me off, it will have been Allah's will.

Before dawn, I make my decision. Despite the pain, I manage to get up and leave the bedroom in silence, closing the door gently behind me. It's still night. The muezzin has just chanted the first call to prayer. In the *zawleru*, the guard sleeps soundly, snoring his head off. I put on my black coat and, taking nothing with me, silently open the back door and plunge into the dark night.

I have no precise plan. I don't know where to go. I know only where I cannot return. Neither my mother nor my father, nor my uncles, will be of any help to me. I have no friends. Not enough money. Nowhere to take refuge. But this is what I have to do. Leave as soon as possible. Go far from here, far from everything. Before daybreak, I have to put as much distance as possible between me and Moubarak, between me and that compound.

VI

My father stands up brusquely from his armchair, he's mad with rage and points an accusing finger at me.

"Tell me the truth, right now. Don't lie to me, you little slut. I know you went to Gawaza! Who do you know in Gawaza? A man, is that who? Now my daughter has lovers!"

"No, Baaba! It's just that . . ."

"It's your mother! Is she the one who took you there?" he shouts.

"No!"

"All right, then! I'll get the truth out of you one way or another," he says, trembling with rage.

I've witnessed my father's uncontrollable anger before, but I've never seen his face so vicious. He is so indignant that he gives me no opportunity to explain, to tell him everything I've suffered at the hands of Moubarak.

"I'll kill you!"

My family searched for me in the days after my flight, until discovering by great coincidence that I was in Gawaza, a small village near Maroua.

The day I deserted the conjugal house, with no precise destination in mind, I hadn't imagined the consequences of leaving, for me or for the rest of my family. With no plan, I took the first bus that arrived. In the streets of the small town, I entered without hesitation the first compound I came across. For a month, I shared the daily life of my hosts, a rural family whose wife, Djebba, kind and welcoming, offered me friendship and protection. Without asking me any questions for fear of embarrassing me, she nursed my wounds and boiled medicinal barks that she encouraged me to drink. The care provided by Djebba and her family allowed me to forget my misfortunes temporarily. The legendary hospitality of *pulaaku* helped me feel welcome. I knew that I could stay for as long as I liked; I was part of the household.

Meanwhile, my family was wondering what had happened to me. Moubarak had simply told them we had an argument. My family mobilized to search for me. All of them, torn between worry and anger, sought out any information that might lead to me, and then one day a family friend remembered having made the journey to Gawaza in the company of a woman who looked like the one in the photo they'd circulated. My escape came to an end with the interruption of Goggo Nenné in my new life, followed by Uncle Yougouda.

My uncle brought me back to the house *manu militari* and sat me in the living room, demanding that I wait there under the strict surveillance of my aunt until my father came back from the market. My mother came and held me in her arms for a long time. Her face was pale and her features haggard. Scrawny, she floated in her blouse. Thirty-five years old, worry had aged her ten years in a month. Contemptuous of her torment, my father had added to it, accusing her of being directly responsible for my disobedience.

"Oh! Hindou, what have you done? Have you no pity for me?" I burst into sobs.

"Moubarak savagely beat me that night. I was so afraid, but I knew that if I came back here, you would just send me home immediately," I justified.

"Of course we would have sent you home," Goggo Nenné stated severely. "You are not the first nor the last woman to be hit by a man. That's no reason to disappear like that. You would surely have found a solution. You are not a dead leaf at the mercy of the wind. You have a family to protect you."

"But you would have just told me to *be patient.*"

"Which is normal. Patience is a divine prescription. It is the first response. It is the solution to everything."

"Once, my husband punched me and it knocked me out. I passed out onto the *canari*, the jug where we store water to keep it cold. It broke beneath my weight and made a deep gash in my arm. Without a care, Moubarak left and didn't come back until the early morning. I woke up in the middle of the night, ants all over my hair, my body on fire, and my pagne drenched in coagulated blood. I called for you, my aunt, and I confided in you. You simply encouraged me to be patient. I also confided in my mother-in-law, and she, too, demanded that I be patient."

"And that's why you decided to leave?" Goggo Nenné asked in a scornful tone. "Bravo, you found the solution!"

I said nothing, I merely lifted my blouse, exposing my back to reveal the large lingering bruises. With time, they'd taken on a darker hue, which provoked a stupefied cry from my mother.

"Oh! Hindou, what did he do that with? Why didn't you say anything to me?"

"What did you do to Moubarak for him to hit you with such ferocity?" my aunt asked coldly. "May Allah protect you. Frankly, you and your husband deserve each other. Spare us the details."

"I don't want to be patient anymore," I sobbed. "I've had enough. I'm tired of enduring, I've tried to bear it but it's just not possible anymore. I don't want to hear *patience* one more time. Never say *munyal* to me again! Never again with that word!"

"You have put up with too much, Hindou. More than you should have, perhaps," my mother added, comforting me as I sobbed even harder.

"Tell that to your husband, Amraou!" Goggo Nenné concluded coyly, turning back toward my mother.

Now I'm faced with the fury of my father, who won't let me speak:

"So? Who did you go to see in Gawaza? You don't want to say, is that it? Madame thinks she's a big shot now? That she can do whatever she likes?"

The family crisis has gathered everyone together. My brothers are standing in the courtyard, trying to listen to what's being said. My stepmothers are pressed against the window to listen. As for my husband, my father has summoned him, too. He's waiting on a chair on the veranda. Biting his fingernails, he doesn't seem any more reassured than me. For a moment, our gazes meet; he lowers his eyes.

My uncles Hayatou and Yougouda are also sitting in the living room, faces firm, while my mother, next to me on the bench of the accused, shrinks onto the rug, cowering before my father's intransigent anger.

"Are you going to answer me or not?" he grumbles.

Overwhelmed with anxiety, I stammer.

"I apologize."

"You apologize?"

He enters his bedroom like a madman, comes back out with a long whip, and lashes my shoulders. The strikes whistle faintly through the air. Anxiety, which has strangled me since this morning, transforms into sheer terror. I seek a corner to protect myself from this outburst of violence but my father has lost all control.

"You will tell the truth! Whose man's home were you in? How long have you been having an affair?"

"I swear to you, Baaba, I did nothing! I left because Moubarak beat me."

"You little whore—confess immediately, who were you with? Your husband hit you so you went to find another, is that it?"

The lash of the whip lacerates my skin, ripping my pagne. Moubarak and my uncles watch the whipping, emotionless.

When my father deems the punishment sufficient, he turns his rage back on my mother. She doesn't move, doesn't cry; she takes the lashes stoically, without blinking. Only her eyes, flooded with tears, shine more brightly than usual. She doesn't protect herself. She remains frozen and stares at my father with an air of defiance commensurate with the mute anger churning in the depths of her heart. The entire compound holds its breath. Finally my uncle Yougouda, without moving, intervenes:

"That's enough! Don't strike her in front of her child!"

My father, after a final kick, throws down his whip and wipes his face, dripping with sweat, then takes a sip of water. Still just as furious, he addresses my mother:

"You're worthless! I repudiate you."

"No!" Uncle Hayatou cuts in. "Do not repudiate her. It's not her fault."

"She's the one who spoiled that child. She's the one who gave in to all her whims! She must have known about everything."

"You already set her straight. She understands. *Munyal*. Patience."

"I had no idea, with Allah as my witness," my mother explains. "But you can repudiate me if you like. I will in fact leave, even if you don't. I, too, am tired. I, too, have endured too much, tolerated too much."

"Amraou, be quiet and go back to your apartment. You won't be going anywhere and you won't be repudiated," Uncle Yougouda interjects. "We can never have enough patience. He who is patient will never regret it, and no one is more patient than Allah. When we are parents, we must shoulder the burden. You, too, Boubakari, must be patient."

My father calms down. Relieved to be able to reconcile with his favorite without losing face, he takes a seat and, facing her, adds in a gentle voice:

"You may go back to your apartment."

My mother, without glancing at me or at him, stands up without a word, readjusts her veil, and leaves the room with a haughty air. I am aware, knowing her, that she leaves only out of pride. And I also know that, as usual, my father will make her come back, using all the necessary persuasion, countless promises, and expensive gifts. Uncle Hayatou then calls for Moubarak.

"I know all about your behavior, too. Watch yourself, Moubarak! You'll get nowhere behaving like a lowlife. We know you mistreat your wife, that you take drugs and drink. It's not wise. Beyond the fact that she's your wife, she's also your cousin, and you owe her protection. Let this be the last time that I hear you've hit her. When we marry a stranger, we owe her respect. When we marry a member of our family, we owe her double the respect. Are you trying to break up the family? You are not innocent in what has happened here."

"Of course, my uncle. I understand and will be better."

"I did not give you my daughter for you to mistreat her, Moubarak. If you don't want her anymore, simply send her back," my father says harshly.

"I apologize, my uncle. I will not mistreat her again, *wallahi*, I swear in the name of Allah. Of course I love her. And I am very happy with her. I truly regret what has happened."

"In any case, you've been warned, and for the last time," my father adds firmly.

Uncle Hayatou then turns toward me:

"This story has been buried once and for all, Hindou. Know that we are severe in order to protect you from the turpitudes of this life and the next, because you are our daughter, and we care for you. Only a person who loves you will reprimand you. The others will remain indifferent to your wanderings. I hope you will get yourself together from now on, respect your husband and preserve your honor and that of your family. If he hits you again, come to tell me. If he offends you, do not hesitate to inform me. I will find a radical solution. You heard what your father said. If your husband does anything to you, we are your defenders. Do not seek out solutions alone. Now, Moubarak, get your wife and take her back home. I repeat, all of this is your fault. You spend all day doing who knows what and come back late at night threatening your wife. Come to see me tomorrow at my office. It's high time you took on some responsibility."

My father had already moved on to other things, busy speaking enthusiastically on the phone. I followed Moubarak without uttering a word. When I entered my bedroom sobbing my head off, he simply closed the door gently behind me. A few minutes later, he came back, bandaged my wounds, and handed me a few pills that I swallowed immediately before curling up in my bed. Only a groan from time to time broke the silence. We said nothing. Life resumed its normal course.

I had been married for a year at that point. And I was pregnant. The night of the rape and my flight to Gawaza marked the beginning of a life clinging to my insides. Neither my anguish nor my bitterness nor my father's magisterial punishment could dissuade the child from growing in my womb. It seemed determined to live.

VII

I've changed. They say I'm sick. Maybe it's true. I don't know. I'm too tired to think about it. For nine months, I've suffered through my melancholy in addition to my pregnancy. After so much violence, my nerves are raw. I jump at the slightest sound. My stomach is permanently in knots. I have a constant ball of anxiety at the bottom of my throat. The sadness of those first days was replaced by silence and depression. I don't speak anymore, don't leave my bedroom, the curtains are always drawn. I have no more energy. And even Moubarak's kindness, which has slightly tapered off, leaves me indifferent. My pregnancy is difficult; I can't stand the nausea. I've become anorexic and eat almost nothing.

I've changed. Now I hear voices. That started the day of the birth. Goggo Nenné, who during my seventh month came to live with me because of my extreme weakness, accompanied me to the maternity ward. The contractions grew stronger and stronger, gripping my abdomen. I was sitting in a bed waiting for the delivery. By my side, my aunt whispered a few final words of advice to me:

"Patience, *munyal*, Hindou! You've heard it before. A Fulani doesn't cry when she gives birth. She doesn't complain. Don't forget. At every moment of your life, you must master yourself and remain in control. Do not cry, do not shout, do not even speak! If you cry during your first birth, you will cry during all the others. If you shout, your dignity will be tarnished. There will always be someone in the neighborhood to call you a coward. We grit our teeth, but we do not bite our lips. If you bite your lips, you might pierce through them when you're in intense pain without even realizing it. It's Allah's will that we give birth in pain, but you can't put a price on a child. Patience! It's because of this pain that we say birth is the jihad of women. It is thanks to this pain that we go directly to Paradise if we die during childbirth. It's because of this pain that a child will always be in debt to its mother."

In my aunt's voice, I heard my father's voice, superimposed, speaking the same words. *Munyal, munyal!* Patience.

I didn't cry. I didn't shout, nor shed a single tear. I didn't complain even when my aunt gave me the traditional scalding bath and massaged me vigorously in the hot water to help me heal as quickly as possible.

"*Munyal!* Listen to my advice, Hindou! A new mother who isn't washed correctly will immediately catch an incurable disease. A new mother has a delicate and vulnerable body. She requires massages and scalding baths. Not warm—scalding. The water must be brought to boiling. You must also eat porridge, warm soups, and a lot of meat and milk."

I let it happen without saying a word. My detachment surprised my aunt. As did my disinterest faced with the newborn.

It's a girl. They say she's beautiful and looks like me. In an effort to redeem himself, Moubarak gave the little girl my mother's name. Such a considerate son-in-law!

I've changed. They say I'm possessed. That a malevolent jinn haunts me. It's normal, a young new mother has a fragile, defenseless body. It's too tempting for an evil spirit to pass up. That's nothing new. My family has started to worry.

I've changed. I'm not sick. The others are getting worked up for nothing. I'm simply oppressed. Why won't they let me breathe? I'm suffocating in the darkness of this bedroom. They say I'm crazy. That worries me a little. Am I really? All these people swarming around me make me anxious. Their inquisitive looks. Their opinions about my state turn more and more decisive. I'm afraid of the horrors they reel off with certitude. I'm worried. Have I changed? They say I'm crazy! Speakers transmit the Quran throughout the house. There's noise. Far too much. It makes my head buzz. Too many people speaking at the same time. I shout to make myself heard. I yell for them to stop that racket pummeling my skull. They look at me with sadness in their eyes. I must really be possessed! It's not noise, it's simply the psalmody of the Sacred Book.

They say I'm crazy and that I've changed. How long have I been in my bedroom, closely monitored by my aunt or my mother? How many prayers have the marabouts muttered over my head? How many liters of holy water have they spritzed me with, forced me to swallow? How many liters of that concoction made from *gaadé* roots have they made me drink? How many kilos of herbs have they burned for me to inhale the fumes?

I feel like I'm suffocating, searching in vain for air and unable to breathe. Unable to see anything around me but phantoms. Unable to stand on my feet. Unable to absorb any information. I exist without existing.

I want to scream without opening my mouth, cry without shedding tears, sleep without ever waking up.

They say I'm sick and that I shouldn't move. They even say I've become dangerous. This jinn that possesses me must be male, because I can no longer stand the sight of my husband nor the rare sight of my father or my uncles. This jinn must be in love with me! They say that he probably invaded my body when I was younger. Surely during a visit to my grandparents' house. There's a large baobab tree in their house. And everyone knows that jinns live in baobabs.

They confirm that I'm crazy. They're tying me down to the bed. They say I'm trying to flee. It's not true. I'm just trying to breathe. Why won't they let me breathe? Or see the light of the sun? Why do they deprive me of air? I'm not crazy. I don't eat because of the ball at the bottom of my throat, because my stomach is so knotted that not even a drop of water can find its way down there. I'm not crazy. I hear voices, but not those of jinns. I hear the voice of my father. The voices of my husband and my uncle. The voices of all the men in my family. *Munyal, munyal!* Patience! Don't you hear them too? I'm not crazy! I only take my clothes off to better breathe in all the oxygen of the earth. To better smell the scent of flowers and feel the cold breeze on my bare skin. For too long, so much fabric has smothered me from my head to my feet. From my feet to my head. No, I'm not crazy. Why won't you let me breathe? Why won't you let me live?

SAFIRA

*Patience is an art
that is learned
patiently.*

GRAND CORPS MALADE

I

Patience, *munyal*, Safira! Remember, you mustn't let anyone suspect your resentment. Don't let them sense your sadness, your rage, or your anger. Don't forget. Be composed! Practice self-control! Patience!"

I fight back my tears, look up to the sky to keep them from falling. My aunt continues:

"All these woman will scrutinize you. They will stare you down in order to catch a glimpse of your despair or hostility toward them. Without exception, they will all be waiting for the moment when you slip up. Everything will play out at that moment. If you give them even a hint of your pain, they will mock you. If you falter for a second, your co-wife will get the upper hand forever. A woman has no worse enemy than another woman! Do not give them the opportunity to speak ill of you. Have self-control, stay strong, do not falter."

"*Munyal!*" a friend of my mother added. "It's when things are hardest that you need to be patient. Remain stoic faced with this hardship. No one, Safira, no one can know that you are sad. Jealousy is a shameful sentiment. You are too noble to feel it—right?"

My husband has taken a new wife.

"Seduce him with your generous conduct, your agreeable presence, your delicious cooking. Show him that no woman will ever be able to surpass you. The advantage of polygamy is that it allows you to test his love and your power over him. You are his first wife. All those who follow will never be as precious as you. None of them will be able to live what you have lived. None of them will be able to give him children as you have given him. You are the favored one, and you will always remain so. His first wife! The *daada-saaré*! You will share him from now on, of course. But has a man ever belonged to a single woman?"

For the past few minutes, the blaring horns of the cars entering the large compound have resounded amid a deafening racket of drums and the trumpets of griots who passionately sing the praises of Alhadji Issa and his new wife. The women unleash their youyous. The young bride's family announces her triumphant arrival exuberantly, vehemently.

I fend off my tears and jump up.

"Where are you going, Safira?" Halima, my dear friend, whispers to me, just as distraught as I am.

"To the bathroom."

"Keep yourself together. I know it's not easy, but hang in there, I'm with you."

In the mirror I see a pale face under ostentatious makeup. My eyes are ringed with dark kohl, eyeliner, and mascara, and my lips outlined with a bright red. Head low, I lean on the sink and try a final time to appear composed. I must not cry, for the eyes always betray the weakness of the heart, no matter how hard we try to cover it up.

I put on the new pagne Halima just brought back from the dressmaker. A brilliant scarlet pagne made from fine silk. Memories of my recent trip to Dubai, my golden jewels gleaming in the artificial light of the fluorescent lamps. Just like the new bride, I imagine, my hands and legs are tattooed with black henna arabesques. I must appear in my most beautiful jewelry to stoically endure a celebration that I must work not to suffer through. No, I will not resign myself to being a sacrificial victim.

Through the window, I hear the griot praising the beauty of my new co-wife. These words pierce my heart:

"I will describe Ramla for you, the bride, Ramla the beautiful, the brunette, the gracious, incomparable to any other woman. She is three parts black, three white, three plump and three slim. Black gums, jet-black hair, black eyes. White teeth, white eyes, white palms. A slim waist, like a wasp. A thin neck, like the daughter of a giraffe. Slender feet. Plump cheekbones, arms, and buttocks. Ramla, the beautiful, the incomparable . . ."

My aunt Diddi knocks at the door and wrests me from my morose thoughts:

"Safira, what are you doing in there?"

"I'm coming!"

"Your in-laws are waiting for you to finally welcome the bride."

I repeat in a murmur: "I'm coming."

"What are you doing in there, Safira?"

My breathing is shallow when I pray quietly to Allah. With no conviction that my prayer will be granted. My God, how am I supposed to face that girl, barely older than my own daughter, who has the right to take my husband from me? How can I bear it? How can I act composed as custom requires of me? What to do so as not to lose face?

I fight back my tears and lean under the tap. I take a sip of water, and breathe deeply several times to calm the hellish rhythm of my heartbeat. Then I leave the bathroom with a determined step.

My apartment, which has always seemed large and luxurious, suddenly seems very cramped: there's hardly room to breathe. I would give anything to be elsewhere. Anywhere else.

Everyone is here, family and friends. They seem sad, sincere for the most part. I can't believe it's real, that what I've feared for years has finally come true and now I'm living out my worst nightmare. I wish I could open my mouth and release my rage. I wish I could wake up to find that it was nothing but a bad dream. Instead, surrounded by people, I advance toward the door, splendid, haughty. No, I will not let myself be belittled. I pointedly lift my head and flash a radiant smile at my sister-in-law, who's waiting for me on the veranda. Then, in a confident voice, I say:

"Congratulations, older sister. We finally have a new wife! *Barka!* Bring me to see and welcome our new bride, our *amariya.*"

The women flooded into Alhadji Issa's large apartment. My family, cross-legged on the rug, form a semicircle around me. My co-wife's family does the same. Opposite me, they carefully position the young bride, who has just emerged from the conjugal bedroom. She is completely veiled under a gleaming alkibbare, but underneath, I glimpse a pagne as sparkly as my own. I have time to appreciate the beauty of her henna tattoos, the purity of her complexion, the slenderness of her hands. She keeps her head lowered and the hood of her coat entirely covers her face.

My sister-in-law, my husband's eldest sister, begins:

"Safira, we present your new bride."

"A welcome event, truly."

"She is your sister! Your little sister, your daughter, your wife. You must educate her, give her advice, show her how the compound operates. You are the *daada-saaré*. You will always remain so, even if your husband marries ten others, and that's a heavy responsibility. Safira, the *daada-saaré* is the mistress of the household. If the house lives in harmony, it's thanks to her. She enjoys great respect as a result. But if, on the contrary, there is discord, then it will be her fault. And you, Safira, are the *daada-saaré*. As such, prepare to tolerate everything. The *daada-saaré* is the punching bag of the family. She is the pillar of the house and the entire family. It's up to her to make the effort, to be tolerant. She must practice self-control and *munyal*. Patience, Safira! You are the *daada-saaré, jiddere-saaré*. *Munyal, munyal...*"

She turns now toward the young bride:

"Ramla, you are now Safira's little sister. Her daughter, as she has become your mother. You owe her obedience and respect. You will entrust yourself to her, ask her advice, and follow her orders. You are the youngest. You will not take initiative pertaining to the management of the compound without the advice of your *daada-saaré*. She is the mistress of the house. You are only her little sister. You will take on the thankless tasks. Absolute obedience, patience before her anger, respect! *Munyal, munyal...*"

I acquiesce with a nod of the head, a half-smile on my lips. Right now, I wish I could skin my sister-in-law alive, who, I know, is not very pleased with my disappointment. How many times over the years has she reproached me for monopolizing her brother? How many times has she complained about our intense complicity? The anger I feel galvanizes me and gives me new energy.

One of my co-wife's parents begins speaking:

"Hadja Safira, you are the *daada-saaré*. Today we entrust our daughter to you. You must take her under your wing and teach her to be a wife. You must protect her and help her. She is your little sister, your daughter. We entrust her to you more than to your husband, for, even against him, you must defend her."

"Yes, of course!"

Another woman, entirely veiled, adds:

"One day, a man came to see the Prophet and said to him: 'O servant of Allah, I'd like to live with you; if you accept, we will never argue. But the day we do, we will never reconcile, for I hold a grudge!' The Prophet, in his great wisdom, responded: 'Go away, I will not live with you.' Another man came to see him and said: 'O servant of Allah, I would like to live with you! We will argue often, but we will reconcile immediately.' And the Prophet agrees: 'Yes! I will live with you, for God does not like disputes that go on and on.' All this to show you, Safira and Ramla, that when you live together, disagreements and misunderstandings will occur. Even the teeth condemned to live alongside the tongue cannot help but bite it from time to time."

A lot of other advice is given to the new bride. Finally, I'm able to withdraw. I leave my husband's apartment, ceding my place to another. She will be the only one there for a week. Then we will begin to take turns, sharing our husband.

It's over. My husband's apartment is off limits to me. I must now await my *walaande* before entering, just as I must wait my turn to see him and speak to him. My heart is heavy: I'm no longer alone in my house. I'm no longer a beloved spouse. I am now just a wife, one of the wives. Alhadji Issa, my love, is no longer my lover. Starting tonight, he will be in the arms of another, and just imagining it makes me feel faint. No matter what they say, nothing will ever be the same again. Can a man's heart really be shared between two women?

Halima gently pinches my arm, and while my family sits in the living room discussing what has just happened, passing around the bride's jewels to better scrutinize her father's riches, eyeing up the members of her family, whose full veils are already the subject of great curiosity, I take refuge in my bedroom, where I burst into tears.

Halima comes to my aid and carefully locks the door:

"Oh, Safira, don't give them the satisfaction. You've kept it together up till now. They'd all love to see you dejected. Don't let them gossip about your sadness. The bride is here, of course! But will she stay? It's up to you to make him regret his decision and come back to you. The most important thing is not the wedding, but what comes next. Nothing guarantees that she will be a good wife, that she will even be able to stand him. After all, you've been here nearly twenty years. And it hasn't always been easy!"

"She's so young, so beautiful!"

"How do you know whether she's beautiful, Safira? Her head was lowered and covered in black fabric! You're out of your mind! Your jealousy is playing tricks on you."

"She's so pale, almost white!"

"That doesn't mean she's beautiful. You glimpsed her skin tone and decided she's beautiful based on that. You have pale skin, too.

But who cares. Pale skin isn't what makes you beautiful. Tell me, Safira, where's the dump where we toss the dark-skinned women, so I can go throw myself out, with my horrible dark skin," she adds, laughing, to lighten the mood.

"I can't stand it! I can't share him. It's even worse with a woman so young. She's even younger than our first daughter. How can my daughter be my rival? How can I fight my daughter? I'm already so old!"

"You're thirty-five. You're not old. At our age, in certain cultures, women are still not married. I'm not saying this to flatter you, Safira, but you are still young and beautiful. Her marriage has nothing to do with you."

"Everything was going so well between us. Why did he have to go and ruin it?"

"Because he's a man, my dear. You're getting upset over nothing, truthfully. He will sleep with her and then as soon as her novelty has worn off, he'll come back to you."

"I can't stand it. Even the idea that . . ."

"Don't be naive, Safira! Who told you he's been faithful all this time? Go wash your face. I hear your sister-in-law's shrill voice. She'll be only too happy to see your tears."

To my great surprise, my husband called for me a few hours later. Before going, I made sure to wash my face with cold water to erase any trace of tears, and then I carefully reapplied my makeup. Our gazes met for a moment. He was the first to lower his eyes. My heart was racing as I sat calmly in an armchair. My anger toward him melted, replaced by an immense sadness. I was cruelly aware of my feelings for all those years and the pain of knowing that, for him, the page had turned. I was no longer the woman he loved and cherished. I was nothing more than a wife among wives. The mother of his children.

For twenty years, I had invested in our love. All that remained of that love now was what we felt for our children.

Sitting on a couch, he was carelessly dressed in a casual boubou I didn't recognize. He barely looked at me. Already, I was invisible to him. His gaze didn't linger on my new pagne or on my henna tattoos. He called for the new bride and asked her to sit down next to me. She kept her head lowered, still veiled. A heavy silence settled in, disturbed only by the sighs and tears of the young woman.

With pride, Alhadji said: "Safira, I present to you your sister Ramla. I believe you've already met."

"Yes."

"What do you think? She's beautiful, isn't she?"

"Very. May Allah grant you happiness," I said.

"*Amine!* And you, Ramla, you've seen your *daada-saaré*? I know you've already received instructions and advice from your families and from mine. But I still wanted to bring you together tonight to make sure you understand what I expect of you both. It comes down to a single word: 'harmony.' I want absolutely no disorder in my home. I will never allow my household to become a battlefield or a place of discord as so many are. I intend to live tranquilly without headaches or any other issues. My house is to remain a place of quiet and serenity as it always has been. Safira, you know me well. I do not tolerate disagreements or conflicts. I am warning you both, it's in your best interest to get along and make me happy. Is that clear?"

Since neither of us responded, he turned toward me:

"Safira, I will say it again in front of your co-wife. We've been together twenty years, and I haven't been married to anyone else up to this point. I am doing so now not because I'm trying to punish you. I've already told you this. I offered you as many gifts as my new bride, which is not the custom, I could have given you far fewer, but this is to show you the respect I have for you and for our children. I hope that you will be cooperative and worthy of my trust, as you have been for many years."

Turning to his new bride, he continued:

"Ramla, this compound has always lived together in peace. I married you so that I could be even happier. Do not misunderstand me, my first wife's place is intact in this house and in my heart. You will respect her and follow her instructions. If one day you hurt her, know that you will have hurt me, too. You owe her every consideration. If you make me happy through your good behavior, I will not take a third wife."

He stayed quiet for a moment, then concluded:

"Safira, you may go. Good night!"

Silent tears streamed down my cheeks; I was unable to hold them back. Of course, I didn't want my co-wife to see my sadness and distress, but, after a day like today, I couldn't stifle my pain any longer. I had just been dismissed, asked to leave the premises for the mandated week. My husband was already on his feet. Walking ahead of me, he accompanied me to the door without saying anything, closing it carefully behind him. The lights went out one after another. I felt faint. Stepping over the women sitting in my living room, I rushed back to my room and burst into sobs.

II

I'm going to Yaoundé. I have urgent matters to attend to."
"Okay."
"I'm taking Ramla with me."
"What?" I asked.
"You heard me," he says coldly.

The eighth day, it's my turn. My *walaande*! The honeymoon established by our religion is over and now Alhadji must be shared between his new wife and me. I've been preparing to see my husband again.

When he informed me of his intention to take a new wife after twenty years of marriage, he had made a unilateral decision that, he claimed, had nothing to do with me. It was his right; he refused to discuss it. However, I was free to refuse this state of existence and, if I so wished, he could free me. But between his desire to marry again and his desire to keep me, he had already made his choice. He reminded me that it was in my interest to be reasonable and obedient:

"Open your eyes, Safira!" he said. "Polygamy is normal and even necessary for maintaining harmony in the conjugal home. All men of importance have several wives. Even the very poor. For example, your father is polygamous, isn't he? If it's not with me, it'll always be with another. You'll never be alone in a man's home. You should be grateful and thank Allah for having been alone all these years. You've benefited from not having to share in your youth. It's egotistical to be bitter now. Do you think you're wiser than the All-Powerful, who has authorized men to have up to four wives? Are you more important than the wives of the Prophet, who accepted polygamy with dignity? Do you think you're a man, claiming we can't love several women at once?"

The eighth day. It's my turn to be with my husband. He knows it and yet has decided to take Ramla with him on his trip. The eighth day! He enters my apartment cleanly shaved and dressed in a new white *gandoura*, richly embroidered with gold, to inform me coldly of his trip.

I answer feebly: "You're leaving with her?"

"There's no need to repeat what I've just said as if it were abnormal or a shock. You're acting like I've committed a crime. I'll remind you, since you seem to have forgotten, that I've taken you on several trips. You went to Douala barely four months ago. But I don't have time to discuss this. I'm leaving. The flight is in an hour and the airport is far."

"It's my turn tonight! You're supposed to be with me and not still with her, especially after such a long week spent together!"

"It was your turn every day of the last twenty years!" he says. "Don't start with this childishness. Are you not ashamed of begging for another night? We've been married for how long? I see you've understood nothing. I may be polygamous but, until proven otherwise, I am a free man and I'll do what I want. Here's some money for anything that might come up while I'm away," he says, dropping a wad of bills on the rug. "I don't know when I'll be back. I'll call you."

"Why? What did I do for you to hurt me this way? Why are you breaking my heart?"

"Here we go again! Melodrama suits you so well, my word. But look at you, Safira! You look like you're in mourning! Look at how you're dressed. And your eyes? How long has it been since you wore kohl? You think this is how to seduce me? Get ahold of yourself—immediately. I don't have time to discuss this right now, but you are disappointing me enormously. I hoped you'd have more dignity than this. It's like you're the first woman to have a co-wife! Ramla's only been here a week and look at you! Give me a break," he adds, seeing my tears fall. "You're bordering on ridiculous. I'm trying not to get worked up, so, I'll see you soon!"

He turns around, in a hurry to leave. In the deserted living room, the scent of his heady perfume still lingers. I withdraw to my bedroom. Through the window, I see him full of joy, greeting his "sycophants," with whom he's closer than the employees but who aren't quite friends, his men who take care of the compound every day, whether he's there or not. Their role? Bring him the latest news of the neighborhood, keep him company, be available for confidential or important errands. In a good mood, my husband orders the driver to bring his nicest car, his latest acquisition, which arrived a month ago from Dubai. I see him whisper a word to his lackey who quickly leaves and comes back a few minutes later with his new wife. I cry silently without trying to hold back my tears.

Ramla is beautiful. I see her in the light of day, which illuminates her silky skin. She's dressed in a new embroidered pagne and wearing magnificent golden jewelry. She must have had her black henna tattoos redone, because the designs stand out nicely on her pale skin. Elegant, well made up, she enters the back of the car with no timidity to join her husband, who is beaming with happiness. However, Ramla looks sad.

I remain standing there in front of the window long after the car has disappeared. My youngest daughter, Nadia, wrests me from my thoughts:

"Maman! Maman, what are you looking at?"

"Nothing. Go play and leave me alone. I need to rest."

"I saw the new auntie. She left with Baaba."

"I know, go play!"

"She's beautiful; she's kind, too. When I went to her apartment, she gave me a cookie. Her apartment is very pretty."

"I'm tired, Nadia. Behave! Go play outside with your brothers, please. I have a headache."

"Do your eyes hurt too? They're red. Maybe you caught *appolo*, conjunctivitis, like I had before."

"Yes, that's it! You see? I caught *appolo*. That's why I need to rest. You remember how much it hurts. Go play with your doll. If you're good, I'll give you a present when I wake up."

After an hour spent pacing in my room, my sadness transformed into rage. I will not let him mock me like this! No, I will not let myself be humiliated all over town. As I come to grips with my situation, my indignation and hostility intensify. As soon as everyone finds out he's taken off with his new bride on the eighth day, that she's already become his favorite, I'll lose the respect everyone has for me. I won't stand for it!

I imagine the two of them sitting side by side in first class on the plane, en route to the capital. I imagine the envious looks of the other men at the sight of this bride, so young and so beautiful. I see his eyes gleaming with pride. I see myself at his side, not even six months ago. I was so happy and peaceful then on that plane, far from imagining that I would soon be replaced.

My bedroom mirror reflects my image. The pagne I'm wearing, although of great value, does not flatter me. My face is pale and, in the space of a few days, creases have lined my forehead. A few faint wrinkles already appear at the corner of my lips. Six pregnancies have ruined my formerly flat stomach. My arms are no longer as slender and, of course, I'm a few kilos too heavy. I'm barely thirty-five but, over the course of a week, I seem to have aged ten years. I feel so old. By contrast, I picture Ramla, young and so well mannered. I compare her skin with mine, now dull. I remember her finely braided hair falling down to her waist, and I recall her delicate profile, her full mouth, and her straight nose. How am I supposed to take on such a rival?

I end up calling my brother on the phone, then my mother, and finally Halima. I beg them all to come see me as soon as possible. I'm not going to let it happen; it will be difficult but I will fight it every way I can. I decide to hold a council of war. I summon my general staff.

My brother Hamza arrives first. In a cold voice, I explain my decision. He goes to see our distant uncle, the marabout who lives in the village of Wouro Ibbi. I don't simply want to coax back my husband's feelings and be his favorite. I want my uncle to rid me of my rival. It is out of the question for me to share my husband.

"Tell him I'm prepared to do anything. I'll give him anything he wants. I'll do anything he asks. I just want her to leave! Immediately! For Alhadji to repudiate her! Stay there as long as it takes. There are five hundred thousand francs in this envelope. Spend it all if you have to. Even if he asks for a sacrificial ox, do it! The cost doesn't matter. I want her gone! Remember her name, the names of her mother and father, too, so he can cast a spell on them all."

"I understand, big sister. Don't worry. I'll do whatever is necessary."

"I trust you. Stay there as long as it takes."

An hour later, my mother discreetly walks through the door in her turn. As soon as I see her, I say, quite aggressively:

"Diddi, figure something out, she has to go."

"Safira, be careful! Don't do harm unto others, it can come back to bite you. Beware of *siiri*! Cursing people is a dangerous practice."

"I don't care. I'm prepared to do anything. I refuse to be humiliated."

"Polygamy is not shameful for a woman. *Munyal!* Get ahold of yourself, Safira."

Barely containing my anger, I tell her in a muffled voice: "Alhadji left with her for Yaoundé."

"What? He left today? With her? Already?"

"Apparently the seven legal days weren't enough for him. He's gone to find tranquility elsewhere—with her and without sharing."

"Leave it alone. It's the lure of novelty. Soon that will be over, and he'll see that you're the one he loves. He's always lived with you, and he'll come back to you even more in love than ever. Just be a little patient."

"I don't want to be patient," I say, very irritated. "Don't ever talk to me again about *munyal*. I won't hang around for his caprice to wear off, as you say. I don't have time to wait for some hypothetical moment. I want her gone immediately. I want you to cast a *karfa* over them, for this spell to separate them, for them to break it off in Yaoundé. I want him to regret this marriage. I'm prepared to lose everything I have for it. I will not lose my honor."

"You're scaring me, Safira," she says. "How could you change like this in just one week? Let me tell you a story. Listen to me. This is what they tell married women when they feel the need to resort to dark magic.

"One day, a woman goes to see a marabout and says to him: 'I need my husband to love me and be faithful to me.' The marabout asks her to bring him back three whiskers of a lion in order for him to make an amulet. The woman reflects and for a long time considers how to approach a lion's den without putting herself in danger. She gets the idea to place fresh meat a few feet away from the den and take off rapidly as the lion eats. Each day, she does the same thing, getting a little closer to the beast every time. After a while, the lion becomes used to it and starts to wait for her. Then he lets her pet him, and she is able to tame him. Thus, she manages to pluck his whiskers without the wild cat showing any sign of hostility.

"When she brings the marabout what he asked for, he sends her away with these words: 'If you were able to tame a lion, then your husband, a mere man, does not exceed your powers. Do exactly the same thing with him and he'll be yours forever. If you were able to procure these whiskers, you have the best qualities a woman can possess: patience and cunning. Handle your husband as you would a child. Tame him like the lion you tamed. Be patient, cunning, intelligent, and he will never leave you. That is the secret to keeping a husband. No amulet is worth as much.'"

"Please, Diddi, stop! I already know this story. It was told to me on my wedding day. They went on and on about it. Every woman who came gave me this advice. Sometimes the lion was a viper, sometimes a hyena, but it was always the same story. Don't you understand what I just told you?" I say, exasperated. "I told you, he left with her on a trip when she's only just arrived, and before leaving, he denigrated and insulted me. She's sinking her claws into him and you're talking to me about patience, cunning, and I-don't-know-what!"

Hearing these words, my mother's expression, normally gentle, turns cold. She, too, knows and has suffered the hardships of polygamy. In fact, she still does. My father, since his marriage to a twenty-year-old, has eyes only for his new spouse. At barely fifty, my mother was relegated to the background. Now my father completely ignores her. The newcomer scorns her and has no shame going to my father's apartment at all hours, whether it's her *defande* or not. The only time my mother dared to rebel, my father berated her with so many insults in front of her rival that she swore to ignore him forevermore. For the last five years, my mother has had no *walaande* and watches, powerless, as her co-wife completely monopolizes her husband.

"Diddi, listen to me. I don't want to end up like you. This girl is already his favorite after a week of marriage."

"Do you have money? I'll go tonight and consult the imam at

the great mosque, Oustaz Sali. You need prayers and sacrifices. Who knows? Perhaps her family has already done something and your husband is bewitched."

"We should have done this as soon as we heard of his plan. Perhaps then we would have been able to stop all of this."

"I see that now. I should have thought of it then. Don't worry, I'll take care of it."

"Don't back down from anything!"

"What do you mean by that?"

"I want them divorced! Or else, for her to leave forever, for her to go insane or die! Those are the options! Don't just go see Oustaz Sali. Find at least three other marabouts."

"For her to die? Oh no, Safira! You wouldn't go so far as murder?" she reacts, frightened.

I insist, fists clenched: "I don't want to end up like you. If she won't leave, let her die!"

Halima doesn't hide her indignation when I tell her about that morning's scene with Alhadji, then my conversation with my mother.

"So he left with her! And on top of that, he insulted you!"

"He did worse. He told me that he didn't care what I felt, and that I was ridiculous for crying. I hope that plane crashes to the ground!"

"Shhh, Safira! You shouldn't say things like that. He is, after all, the father of your children, and you love him, no matter what you say. You can't honestly wish for his death!"

"I'd prefer him dead than in the arms of that girl. If you had seen her this morning looking so holier-than-thou."

"So you saw her? What's she like?"

"Young and beautiful."

"Like you, then. Like all the wives of rich men."

"When he married me, yes, I too was young and beautiful. Today, I feel old. And he's so young that he needs a wife the same age as our daughters."

"Old at thirty-five? And him, young at fifty? It's true that men say they can acquire wives until they're ninety years old! So be it! This isn't the time to convince you. You said on the phone that there was an emergency. Sorry I didn't make it over sooner. I was busy with my bastard of a husband."

"What did he do? Stop calling him a bastard. He's a nice man and he's never done anything to you."

"May Allah keep him from ever having the means to do so, may he keep us in poverty and preserve us from riches. Don't be fooled! He's no different than yours. All men are born from the same mother, they're all alike. He just doesn't have enough money to act all macho! Anyway, let's not talk about him. What was it that you wanted?"

I open a drawer and take out a jewelry box, revealing shining jewels. A gold ensemble gifted to me by my husband during a joint pilgrimage to Mecca, years ago.

"I need you to sell this jewelry for me, discreetly. I need money. Lots of money!"

"But why, Safira? What are you going to do with the money? Why do you want to get rid of such magnificent jewels? You love this set!"

"I adored it! It was the symbol of our love. Today, it's nothing more than jewelry. What am I saying, nothing more than gold!

Which is to say money! I have buckets full of jewels. I'm ready to sacrifice everything to win back my husband. Win back the man. Not the love. The love is dead and lost forever. He killed it with his own hands. No! What am I saying? With his penis!"

Halima bursts into resounding laughter, grows serious again, shakes her head and says:

"You're incredible, but be careful! If you start meddling with marabouts and *siiri*, there's no turning back. You risk losing everything, and worse, it could come back to hurt you or your children."

"Tell me, Hali, what do you expect me to do? Sit back and watch that girl, barely older than my daughter, take my husband from me? Lose my house? Risk my children's suffering if I'm repudiated? They're too young to live without their mother. What do you expect me to do, Hali? Sit here with my arms crossed, waiting for him to toss me out? Die of sadness like our friend Mariam when her husband remarried? After my death, as her husband did after hers, Alhadji will use the opportunity to acquire a third wife that he'll move into my apartment, erasing me from his memory forever. We only die according to Allah's will, he'll say! What do you expect me to do? What is allowed? What is off-limits?

"When we're at war, we can't be picky about our choice of weapon. We take what's available to us and march ahead. And that girl? What did she expect when she decided to become the wife of a married man? She thought I'd just let it happen, is that it? I didn't choose to end up here. They haven't left me a choice. I'm defending myself, that's all. I loved him. I did my best to satisfy him. I was a good wife. An excellent mother. I gave him intelligent, healthy children of both sexes. I comforted him, I loved him with all my heart, with all my soul. What more did he want?

I'm not a mean person. They're forcing me to be this way. I didn't choose to wage this war. But have they left me a choice?"

Out of breath, I stand up and drink water straight from the bottle next to me and add:

"What do you want me to do? What is my plan of action? What other options do I have? Do I really have a choice? What is a so-called symbol of love worth from a man I'm on the verge of losing forevermore?"

"How much do you want for it?" Halima concludes, slamming the jewelry box shut.

III

I am the *daada-saaré*. The newcomer owes me a certain deference. She is a calm girl, introverted. I often glimpse a touch of sadness in her eyes that I refuse to see. Hypocrisy.

She seems more at ease with the children and talks with them quite a bit. I don't appreciate that my daughters like her so much, but I can't keep them from going to see their stepmother, for fear of provoking Alhadji's anger. I have to pretend to the bitter end. I will never show this woman how much I detest her.

I am the *daada-saaré*. I explained to Ramla how the main house functions. I helped her settle into our routine. I kept my cool, I was affable. I gave her advice and made myself available to her.

Alhadji has changed, even if he tries to claim the contrary. He is far less composed, doesn't grant me as much time as before. When my turn comes, he is less attentive, seems elsewhere. And it upsets me to see the pills he swallows, those fortifiers and aphrodisiacs he depends on now.

I've gotten used to sharing him. The insomnia at the start of the other's turns, the crying fits and the disgust I feel when he touches me have faded over time, but my determination has not faltered. I still want everything back to the way it was. Ramla simply needs to leave. Above all, she must not become pregnant. Each child she has will only diminish the inheritance of my own. The new offspring will only curb the love their father has for them. I'm obliged to share him—but I don't want my children to have to share him, too! I closely track her cycle. I know when her period starts. And those days, stressed, I surveil, keep watch to see whether she continues her prayers, because if so, that means she's pregnant. My heart unclenches when I see her ignore the call of the muezzin. Then I can breathe easy. At least until her next cycle.

The curses have not worked yet. But my jewels disappear one after another. I spend more and more money. I change marabouts every time I don't see a result, I rush to another as soon as I hear of him. I need money. More and more money to achieve my mystical plans. Time goes on, and Ramla not only hasn't left but even seems to have gained a certain confidence. She's settling in!

I need money and, luckily, it's the time of the *zakat*, the obligatory alms. A period of stress for Alhadji Issa, but fortunate for me because it's the only day of the year when I can replenish my cash flow without drawing attention. For five days, the most destitute from all over the city flock to the house. They spend their days and some even their nights outside the compound, sitting on the ground, in silence. Nothing can dissuade them, not even the scorching afternoon sun. They all wait patiently for the long-awaited distribution to begin. When the heavy gates of the compound open, they all stand up at the same time, speak, shout, jostle one another. The guards roughly push them back, but it doesn't calm their enthusiasm. The women also gather to watch the distribution of bills. Each year, Alhadji entrusts one of his employees with the task of preparing the envelopes sent to the imams, the patriarchs, and the needy. In the morning, before departing, he leaves me one or two million to distribute to the people teeming about outside. I know that I don't have a right to any of the *zakat* money. As Alhadji's wife, I am not allowed to spend it. That's why he doesn't think twice about handing it to me. And, for years, I've distributed that money as I am bound to do. The money I've been taking recently from what he gives me for groceries or, more discreetly, from the pockets of his *gandoura*, no longer suffices. I rip open the envelopes one after the other and take half of their contents, then I carefully reseal them. I bribe the children's Quranic teacher who's in charge of the distribution. I summon him to the living room after Alhadji's departure.

"Malloum, you must go distribute money to the poor outside," I say. "Be wary of a stampede. Remember that last year there were deaths in Alhadji Sambo's courtyard during the distribution of the *zakat*. Alhadji does not want there to be any scandal at his home. Do what you have to do to make these people understand that."

"Yes, Hadja. I always warn them that if they don't settle down, I'll go back inside without distributing any money."

"Good. You are an intelligent boy and you have my support. I'm going to be honest with you. Alhadji gave me two million to distribute. But I'm keeping one million. It's not for me. It's to increase the share going to my own family in need, and I don't want to mention it to Alhadji. You can keep two hundred thousand for your personal needs. It will stay between us."

"Yes, of course, Hadja," says the boy, pleased to take a part of the *zakat* meant for the most impoverished, with my blessing.

"If by chance he asks you, I gave you two million and you distributed it to the rightful claimants. Per usual. Five thousand francs for the women, ten for the men."

"Right away, Hadja. You can trust me."

I am the *daada-saaré*. I'm entitled to a few advantages. And the *zakat* is one of them.

IV

I'm now closely monitoring the replenishment of the house safe.
Alhadji regularly supplies and withdraws money as needed. He
showed us, me and Ramla, how to open it, as well as where he
keeps the keys, in case we need money while he's away. But we
don't have to wait for emergencies—I know how to create them.
I've learned cunning and I use it. I often take the children to the
dentist and inflate the bill. I ask doctors to prescribe me medi-
cations for imaginary illnesses and quote a higher price from the
pharmacy on the corner. Bulk products, piling up in the house
storage area, do not escape my overflowing imagination in time
of war. If the employees at the market are shocked by the quan-
tity of oil, sugar, rice, or milk I buy up for the compound, they
keep it to themselves. I am the *daada-saaré* and I still hold power.
It's not a good idea for them to be on my bad side. Besides, I'm
very generous—I protect them. Alhadji doesn't think twice about
the compound's daily expenses because I've always known how to
spend moderately and reasonably. But that was before his second
marriage! Now I'm on the lookout for the slightest opportunity.

One day, I find wads of euro bills in the safe. I know they're
worth a lot of money in comparison with CFA francs, our na-
tional currency. A few weeks ago, to my great displeasure, Alhadji

took Ramla to Paris. I've never been. When I asked why he didn't take me, he simply answered that there was nothing for me to do there. I'm not educated. I barely speak French. Why would I want to go to Europe? That foreign money must be left over from their escapade. Ramla came back with bags full to bursting, and Alhadji brought back only perfume for me and sweets for the children. Just enough to exacerbate my indignation and anger! The curses have still not brought about the intended results, so I'm hatching a plan to create serious marital problems for Ramla. I've just had an idea. An idea so magnificent that I can't help but laugh. I will take the euros from the safe.

As soon as Halima enters my apartment, I double-lock the door. Then I whisper:

"Do you know how much this is worth?"

"Oh my God, Safira! That's a lot of money. Those are euros!"

"How much?" I ask frantically.

"Ten thousand euros! Around six million of our francs. Did you steal them from Alhadji?"

"Tsk tsk, Hali! Remember, theft doesn't exist in marriage. I am simply planning my vengeance. I have no need to spend this money right now."

"What do you intend to do with it, then?"

"You'll see! He called me illiterate and took off to Europe with his new young thing. I'll show him how illiterate I am. Can you hide this money? You're the only one I trust. No one can know. You must be careful."

"I know where to keep it. Don't worry."

"He can be crazy, conceited, stingy. It's possible he'll go search your place, knowing our relationship."

"Trust me, Safi, I'll hide it somewhere he'll never find it."

When my husband realized the money was missing a few days later, he started to rant and rave. He was completely thrown. It was Ramla's turn. Shouts stormed the compound. I immediately understood what was happening, but I didn't flinch. Secretly, I celebrated the awful quarter of an hour my co-wife endured. A few moments later, he summoned me and, calmly, I went to his apartment. He was standing, enraged. Ramla was sitting in an armchair and crying. She barely lifted her eyes when I entered. I sat next to her in a sign of solidarity. To flag our sacred bond in the face of adversity!

"When's the last time you opened the safe, Safira?" he questioned me, furious.

"A week ago, I think. You asked me to take out a million. You were with your brother, if I remember correctly."

"How much money was in the safe? What did you see exactly?"

"I don't know. I didn't count the money. I just took out the million from among the other wads of cash. There were also the jewels I keep there, Ramla's too, and the jewelry you bought for the girls. There were other bills in there too, but I didn't recognize them."

"That money has disappeared. Those are euros, the equivalent of at least six or seven million francs! I brought them back from Europe. You didn't take them by accident? You're the only ones with the keys to the safe. Don't lie to me!"

"Disappeared? I had nothing to do with it, Alhadji, and you know it. Why would I start stealing from you after twenty years of marriage? And if I did, I would obviously take money I can use. Don't involve me in your affairs! Besides, this is the first I've heard about these euros."

Ramla starts to cry even harder. I barely glance at her.

"I didn't take that money," she says, choking.

"I didn't take it either."

"Are you willing to swear on the Quran?" he asks, a strange gleam in his eyes.

Islam is always the last resort to flush out the truth. Swearing on the Book is an extremely serious matter, and it is required only in the very rare cases that justify it. It can bring about grave danger, possibly even expose an entire family to destruction. Even though I'm well aware of his egotism and his particular relationship to money, I didn't expect him to take things this far. So I decide to play dumb:

"Swear on the Quran? You're joking, Alhadji. I would never mess with the Quran!" I say standing up, as indignant as him. "I have children!"

"I can't place my hand on the Quran unless my family gives their permission," Ramla declares in a quiet voice.

"It must be because you know you're not innocent. Go back to your apartments. I'll call for you soon. It's up to you whether you want a scandal or whether you prefer to handle this between us."

"There are also the servants!" Ramla says. "They can steal, too."

Immediately I add: "There are also your close friends who are always here. But of course you would never suspect them."

"You are the only ones with the keys to the safe."

"The keys are always in the same place," Ramla remarks. "They're not even hidden . . ."

"Get out of my sight. I'll call for you soon. Go and think!"

Without exchanging a glance, we go back to our respective apartments. On the inside, I'm celebrating my co-wife's distress, and I have to expend great effort to hide my joy. Finally, she too is experiencing the hardships of marriage.

They've been married less than a year; now their honeymoon is definitively over. And Alhadji's threats leave me indifferent. I'm used to his tirades—and his moods.

Later, Alhadji enters my apartment, followed by two employees. He asks me to leave. Together, they search the apartment from top to bottom. For his prying eyes, they lift the rugs, examine the ceiling, pull the clothes from their hangers, and inspect every trinket, to the children's great horror. I remain impassive.

They do the same in Ramla's apartment. They find nothing, which exacerbates our husband's furor. Then he summons us again.

Ramla's eyes are red from crying. She seems completely overwhelmed. He stares at us for a long time, then begins:

"I trusted you both. All the men in this country hide their fortune from their wives. I've done my best. You want for nothing. How could you steal from me? My question still stands—which one of you took that money? The one who confesses will be pardoned. If you continue to deny, there will be grave consequences, because I will find out. I'll consult the marabouts, I'll alert the police, I'll do everything to find the person responsible. Safira, follow me."

He takes me alone into the second living room.

"So? Do you have anything to say?"

"Have I ever stolen from you over these twenty-two years? Before your second marriage, had you ever lost anything?"

"Don't use this situation to settle your score. We're not discussing my second marriage right now."

"In any event, you were right: I'm illiterate. I don't speak enough French to go to Europe. What would I do with those euros? Where would I go? If I had to steal, I would take money I could use. Remember that I am *illiterate*. I hadn't even heard of that currency before you told me about it! You'd be better off demanding an explanation from those who went to school and are educated enough to go to Paris."

I turn my back on him.

He remains frozen, petrified by my confidence and audacity. Returning to the first living room, I whisper to Ramla in a sneering voice: "Your husband is waiting for you in the second living room."

Unable to get it out of us, more and more aggravated, *our* husband rages, roars, threatens, with no result. Neither Ramla nor I will agree to swear on the Quran, vastly preferring to confront his rage than that of Allah. So, as a last resort, he summons us a final time at nightfall. He doesn't raise his voice. He stares at us for a long time with his cold stare. His inscrutable expression heralds nothing good. Ramla sits on the farthest armchair, terrified. She can barely keep her eyes open, so swollen are they from crying. Alhadji, letting his austere gaze shift between us, questions us harshly:

"So, Safira, do you have anything to say?"

"Nothing."

And I look him right in the eyes.

"And you, Ramla?" he asks, turning to my co-wife.

She doesn't say a word and bursts into tears.

"Well then, I repudiate you both. You are accomplices—you're conspiring against me to steal from me. Get your things, the driver will take you back to your families immediately. I have nothing else to say. You may leave."

Ramla doesn't respond. She stands up without a word and goes back to her apartment. Not even ten minutes later, she walks out and climbs into the car. Calmly, I remain seated.

After my co-wife's departure, his face expressionless, Alhadji looks at me with disdain: "I said I repudiate you both. Your co-wife has already left. What are you waiting for? Go!"

"You're unjust. You're a millionaire and you earned that fortune after our marriage. When I married you, you were a modest but kind man. As the money in your bank account accumulated, your heart hardened. In the beginning, we loved each other! You've decided that I'm no longer enough for you. No, you don't need an educated woman, you need a pretty young thing. I've tolerated it all, and now you accuse me of stealing your euros. Six million francs, Alhadji! What is six million compared with twenty years of marriage and devotion? What is six million compared with the six children I've given you? What is that money compared with all we've lived through together? The jewels you gave me over the years are worth much more than six million. I'll give them to you, but I will not go. I will not abandon my children."

He doesn't say a word. I stand up and leave the room. A half hour later, while I'm eating dinner with the children, the driver enters my apartment.

"Hadja, I'm back."

"And?"

"Alhadji has asked me to tell you that . . . that the car is waiting for you," he concludes, embarrassed.

I comply. It's the only way to preserve my dignity! I can't be this rudely dismissed and stay.

As the car takes me back to my father's compound, I think quickly. My goal has been achieved. I've managed to have Ramla repudiated! But I got burned, too. I'm leaving, and my reputation is at risk. My children are still young, my family is of modest means and depends on me. The driver, who has stayed silent for a while now, cannot stifle his curiosity any longer:

"What's going on, Hadja? Really, forgive me for asking, but I don't understand."

"Money was stolen from the house. Euros. And he blames us. In twenty-two years, not a single franc has disappeared from our house. With you as my witness, Bakari! You've been here for at least ten years."

"It's true, Hadja!"

"It was only once he took a second wife that it happened! Leave me at his elder sister's house. Her husband is my uncle and a dear friend of Alhadji's. Perhaps it would be better for me to see him first."

"That's a good idea, Hadja. But, I beg you, don't tell him that

I took you there. He gave me orders to drive both of you to your parents' houses."

"In any event, my father's compound isn't far from my uncle's. He'll think I walked."

When I enter my sister-in-law's bedroom, I throw myself on the ground in tears. I cry over the suffering of the last few months; I cry over my husband's betrayal and detachment. He's repudiated me over some money. His sister, seeing my tears and imagining the worst, joins me in sobbing and asks me in an anguished voice:

"What's going on, Safira? Is it my brother? Is he dead? Is it one of the children? What's going on? Tell me, please, don't leave me in the dark!"

"No one is dead. Except me. Except my heart, which is broken. Alhadji has killed me from within."

"What happened that's so horrible?"

She gets up and lowers the curtains to hide us from the inquisitive glances of her co-wives and their children. She draws water from the *canari* next to her and hands it to me:

"Here, drink some water to refresh your heart and soul. *Munyal*, patience, Safira! Every problem has a solution. Only death has no way out. Tell me what happened."

"Alhadji repudiated me."

"What? What did you do that was bad enough to make him repudiate you?"

"Why do you think I did something? Why am I automatically to blame? I did nothing wrong. In fact, he repudiated Ramla, too."

"What? Both of you? Is he insane?"

"Perhaps. Alhadji is always crazy when it comes to money. Someone stole from him apparently. He says he's missing money, and he blames us. But you know me. I've never stolen in my life. He asked Bakari to bring us back to our parents' houses. I wanted to come here first. After all, Uncle Sali is my godfather! If my father hears what happened, he'll have a fit."

"Good thinking! You were always an intelligent woman! Even in pain, you're thinking of the family. Oh my God, what's happening to my brother? Such shame! If not for your sake, he should at least protect his children and think of my honor, too! This will bring shame on me in the eyes of your uncle. He might be angry at me for my brother's indignant behavior. When we have such close family ties, we must take every sensibility into account. Oh, my brother! You are killing me, too," she laments, joining her tears with my own.

"What should I do, older sister? It's late. Perhaps I should go back home, to my father's home, I mean!"

"Stay put," she says bitterly. "My brother might have forgotten about *pulaaku,* but I haven't! I will go to see your uncle and bring you home! Home to your husband and children. You were right not to go back to your parents. They would be mortified by the situation. Such shame! Patience, Safira. That's what marriage is about. That's what polygamy is about. I suffer from it, too. Our newest co-wife is a kleptomaniac!"

My uncle took us back in his car and spoke with Alhadji for a long time. My sister-in-law helped me settle back into my ransacked apartment, scandalized by the mess. She tidied what she could, muttering complaints all the while about her brother. She encouraged me once more to be patient. Before leaving, she brought me to my husband, who was in a heated discussion with her own. Since she was older than him, Alhadji had to listen to her. With me at her side, she sat on the rug and said:

"Alhadji, you too must show patience. I am honestly scandalized by your attitude."

"But . . . they stole from me! I'm doing what I have to do. You yourself know that they want for nothing. They have betrayed my trust."

"Even so, you reacted very rashly. How could you repudiate them both?"

"They refused to tell the truth. I know for a fact that they took the money."

"You have no proof!" my uncle says.

"If they are innocent, why did they refuse to swear on the Quran?"

"On the Quran? You've gone mad, my brother," my sister-in-law cries, horrified. "How can you ask your wives to place their hands on the Quran? That could wipe out the entire family. That could kill you, kill your children, kill me, too. That could bring about destruction, horrible illness, misfortune! You know that perfectly well, my brother!"

"When we refused to do it, he said it was proof of our guilt," I say harshly.

"No, my brother! How could you take such risks and trifle with the Quran, over money?"

"Even if you have proof, you didn't have to renounce them," my uncle adds. "You can't joke around with such things. Divorce may be permissible, but it is the action most detested by Allah. A *hadith* teaches us that divorce undermines Allah's throne. We are not supposed to turn to repudiation except in the most extreme cases. We must not trifle with uttering such things. Even if you reconcile immediately afterward, it still counts as a repudiation. The third time, it's finished. Even if you still love each other, even if you find a middle ground, you won't be able to take it back. Do you realize, Alhadji Issa, that you've just racked up a repudiation for each of your wives on a whim?"

"I was truly enraged. It's six million francs, after all, not six thousand! But in any case, I admit, over the years we've been together, Safira has never stolen from me," Alhadji says, softening.

These words manage to win over my heart, and I begin to sob. No! For all these years, I have never stolen. But this time, I was not innocent. More than the need to possess that money, the desire to rid myself at all costs of that co-wife consumed me. It wasn't the woman herself I was angry at. No, it was just my rival. I didn't like what I had become. But had they left me a choice? For a moment, I felt the need to confess everything. To throw the whole truth in their faces. To tell them about my bitterness, even own up to the other thefts that had gone unnoticed. I had a desire to tell them why I needed so much money, to confess my ventures into dark magic. But the survival instinct glued my mouth shut. No one can ever know. My honor is on the line. My honor, and my happiness.

My sister-in-law offered to go fetch Ramla, and Alhadji silently acquiesced. I gritted my teeth. So it wasn't over yet. After she left, while I stayed seated on the rug, he said to me kindly:

"It's okay, Safira. I believe you. Dry your tears. You may go to see your children."

"I ask more patience from you, Safira," my uncle added. "Tears help nothing. *Munyal!* You are the *daada-saaré*! If there is a problem in the compound, you are automatically affected. Patience, Safira! Patience is a tree with bitter roots, but it bears sweet fruit."

"It's true! Safira has always been a patient and good wife. Don't be upset that your things were thrown around or ruined. I wasn't myself. I'll replace everything. Go now!"

Life resumes its course. I take advantage of a trip to Dubai to meet discreetly with a jeweler and, equipped with my ten thousand euros, replace the jewels I sold, careful to buy the exact same kind. As for the remaining money, I plan a trip to Douala for Halima so that she can exchange it for me and put it in a bank account. A secret account, of course; I am now determined to make things happen.

V

"L et's go to your room, quickly! I have important news to tell you!" Halima exclaims excitedly.

My confidante has arrived, and I can tell from her outfit that she's just returned from a trip. She's wearing a pretty, vibrant *pagne wax*, yellowed with dust and very wrinkled. She looks tired, but her entire being radiates pleasure. She moves swiftly down the hallway. I lock the bedroom door behind her.

"Where are you coming from?"

"From the Central African Republic, where else? I went to see my aunt Zeinabou, like I told you. The one who brags nonstop about the marabouts over where she lives. I had to go see for myself. Let me tell you—they are incredible. If we had found them earlier, I think we could have avoided all the useless worries and extravagant expenses."

"Really?"

"Like I said, they're incredible! I'm coming straight from the bus; I haven't even gone back home yet. I was too eager to tell you everything."

"Go on!"

"Ah, you're in a rush too! In more of a rush than a pigeon in love! Is it true what they say about love being as long as an endless road, as deep as a well, as blazing as fire, as painful as being lanced by a spear? It must be!" she adds, bursting into laughter.

"Tell me what you have to say instead of all your philosophizing, I'm listening!"

"Well, when I arrived after two exhausting days of travel, I rested a few days and then Zeinabou and I left to go see the person in question. She had told me that about a year ago, her husband had started to utterly despise her. He had no time for her and everything about her disgusted and agitated him. She had seen several marabouts, prayed, but nothing had worked until one of her friends, a Central African sympathetic to her distress, came to her aid. She's the one who brought her to this miracle worker."

"That good?"

"Go see how her husband follows her everywhere now and runs circles around her like a loyal dog."

"No!!!"

"I went and saw it for myself. One day, when she was complaining about being tired, he even cooked for her. I was shocked. An attentive and loving man, yes, it's possible! But a man who cooks? I couldn't believe it."

"You sure you're not exaggerating like you usually do?"

She throws me a falsely scandalized look while suppressing an immense laugh.

I continue: "Tell me, then! You went to her miracle maker?"

"Yes, I had to cross the forest. An entire day of walking through the undergrowth. In fact, the marabout was a woman. An old, ageless woman. She was so wrinkled and withered that I thought she was going to die on the spot. But such bounty, such sweetness radiates from her being! It's like she's from another world."

"Another world?"

"A parallel world, you could say. In the prime of her life, married and mother to a child, she drowned in the marigot, and when they never found her body, they assumed that a jinn had taken her. It happens all the time. To everyone's surprise, she reappeared in the same place thirty years later. All of her family members confirmed it was her. So she lived among the jinns, and came back with extraordinary powers."

"You believe this story?"

"She's not the first one this has happened to. Take Bappa Djidda, for example. You know, the seer, at the city limits, they say that he, too, was taken by a jinn in Mayo Fergo and lived for a long time among them. That's where his clairvoyance comes from. Apparently, this *mayo*, inhabited by spirits, takes a few children every year too. You know this, don't you?"

"Yes, it's true. People talk about it. And so, you were able to meet her?"

"You should have seen where she lives! She's right in the middle of the tropical forest, but hundreds of people come to consult her, waiting a long, long time, often weeks or even months before she'll see them. I was lucky! She heard that I had come from very far away and immediately brought me in for a consultation."

"So?"

"Strange voices echo in her lair, decipherable only to her. I had goose bumps. She gave me loads of things for you. She saw that you were going through a rough patch. She guessed that the mother of your co-wife had cast spells. She gave me remedies you must use in your bath, but the most important thing is the secret she whispered to me in our final moments. The secret of women. She decided to gift it to me because she said my heart is pure and our friendship solid, which is rare. You're lucky to have me!"

"Stop boasting and share this big secret with me right now. You're tormenting me."

An incredible hope consumed me. Perhaps she had finally found what I needed to get my serenity back.

"She confided that after everything you do to purify yourself, you then need to use the *secret of women*. The thing that forever binds a man to you."

"What is this secret, then?"

"I'm getting to that. Every time you have intimate contact, you must collect the water from the bath you take afterward. This water contains your two secretions bound together. If you make him drink this water after you infuse it with a particular bark, he will be attached to you forevermore. He will no longer desire any other woman. In order to honor your co-wife, he'll have to think of you first. If he can even manage it! And, even if you haven't had contact, even if you have no more bark, make him drink the water from your intimate bath. All the time!"

"Huh? That doesn't seem like a good idea . . ."

"Oh no? Okay. Do nothing, then! Madame has scruples now," she says severely. "But don't come crying to me after."

"Hmmm . . . I suppose I have no other choice!"

"I suggest you start tonight. Put it in his sauce, his tea, his water. Everything that enters his mouth."

"The problem is that he always eats with people, he drinks the same water as them, the same tea . . ."

"So? Too bad for them. Those people will have to drink it too. Maybe in the end, they'll all fall in love with you!" she adds conspiratorially.

"Yeah, yeah. Or maybe they'll fall in love with him since they'll be drinking his secretions, too!"

"Who cares! That'll teach them to always mooch off the meals of the rich. They should stay home and eat the meal of the poor, the *bôk'ko* their wives make, if they want to be spared from drinking it. They're shameless, abandoning their malnourished wives and children to savor delicious meals without moderation while their offspring languish in misery. They'll only be getting what they deserve."

"You're harsh!"

"You think I'm harsh? Someone told me a story the other day about those *souka*, the cronies that hang around Alhadjis. One day, during a traditional celebration, one of those super-rich Alhadjis said, laughing, that he had heard one of his neighbors was pregnant. Everyone agreed, believing Alhadji's words, except one of them who said that a man can't be pregnant and therefore his information must be wrong. Alhadji felt insulted and cast off the impertinent man. The man went back home but, when poverty started to weigh on him, he came back one night to Alhadji's courtyard and affirmed, completely seriously: 'Alhadji, it's incredible, you were right. The neighbor you said was pregnant gave birth today.' And that's how he won back the favor of his master, who allowed him back into his *zawleru*. I died of laughter hearing this story and thinking of the parasites that hang around your home."

"Halima! You made that up!"

"What do you mean I made it up? Anyway, it doesn't matter if they all drink it too. Do it tonight. I'm leaving, I need to go home. And you can bet I'm going to use the same treatment on my own husband. Safira, I'm begging you, don't neglect this advice."

"You know I won't!"

"I suffered two weeks for this. Imagine: I was stung by insects and even by a scorpion. I was covered in rats walking through the forest. And I crossed hundreds of kilometers!"

"I can't thank you enough. Don't worry, I'll do it all. I promise."

VI

This time, I was determined to succeed. I had to drive my co-wife away. But beyond that, now I wanted to be an educated woman—like her! I begged Alhadji to let me enroll in literacy classes, and he agreed, although mockingly. An instructor came to the house to give me lessons a few times per week. I was hardworking and dedicated. Each time my professor left, I would spend hours writing and attempting to read. My children, amused but supportive and proud, helped me as much as possible. Over the months, I made progress. Now I can read and write. I can use my phone to send text messages. All this progress has galvanized me. When Ramla brought up the idea of learning to drive, I jumped at the opportunity and joined her. Alhadji acquiesced, admitting that our driving permits could be useful in case of emergency. But it was the responsibility of our chauffeur to drive us, of course. Although I had no particular problem with Ramla, I continued to despise her. I was obsessed by my desire for her to leave. A co-wife is still a co-wife even if she is kind and respectful. A co-wife is not a friend—and even less a sister. The co-wife's smiles are nothing but pure hypocrisy. Her friendship serves only to lull you in order to better take you down. I stayed on my guard, and I continued to cast spells. I did everything I could to have my husband to myself again. In addition to the "secret of women" Halima confided in me, I also regularly slipped aphrodisiacs into my husband's tea during my *defande* and dissolved sleeping pills in the bottles of water in his refrigerator at the start of Ramla's *defande*. Slowly but surely, our intimate relationship improved. In the privacy of my bedroom, I watched erotic films and subtly rendered myself more sultry, and adventurous. I bought various youth creams from Nigeria and Chad, discreetly sold by women from house to house. I also acquired all the bewitching herbs and *gaadé* supposedly able to reawaken his desire.

And he was overflowing with desire! Every night of my *walaande*, I would discreetly crush Viagra tablets into his drink. I had to leave him exhausted to be sure he wouldn't do anything the next day for Ramla's *walaande*. I act innocent, but in fact I've become a formidable adversary and sometimes use my children or the maids to achieve my ends. I've continued to mount attacks against Ramla. And it all works! I pour grains of sand on her barbecued meat and in the flour for her couscous. I salt her sauce. I slip even more sand into her conjugal bedsheets at the end of my *walaande*. I hide the soap and toilet paper, dirty the towels, and Alhadji complains, unleashing his rage at Ramla without her being able to explain what's happened. She cooks her meals peacefully in the kitchen and I never enter when she's there, so can't possibly suspect me. Of course, the nights when her cooking is inedible, Alhadji knows he can always come to my apartment to eat chicken and pastries. And then my children enter, joyous, and tell him a thousand and one stories while my co-wife sits around waiting. I offer money and gifts of all sorts to the maids to keep them loyal to me. I've also bribed a few of Alhadji's right-hand men so that they'll be on my side and slyly conspire against Ramla.

Like a spider, I spin my web around my innocent co-wife. She always falls into my skillful traps and is then reprimanded by Al-hadji. I know exactly how to push his buttons, what will set him off. He insults her endlessly. Sometimes, I timidly come to her rescue. But I'm gaining ground. The harmony of their relationship is vanishing as my union with him intensifies. I make myself pretty, buy new pagnes. I wear bold undergarments and even sensually wrap my waist in chains of pearls. I buy increasingly risqué nightgowns, and, to my great surprise, it all pleases my husband. I discreetly add extensions to my hair, which I have done regularly. I've also invested in creams and luxury soaps, using all the latest brightening products to make my already pale skin as white as Ramla's. I've procured the strongest incense and the most precious perfumes. The soles of my feet and my nails are always darkened with henna. And my tattoos are redone often with different patterns each time. I have designs done in the most unexpected places: the small of my back, the top of my thigh, even the curve of my breast. Coquettish, I once had his initials done, which flattered his overinflated ego.

During my *defande*, I clean his apartment from top to bottom, making the bed with new silk or fine cotton sheets. I prepare him scented baths, I follow him into the bathroom to chat gaily and rub him with a soft sponge. When he emerges from the bath, I dry him like a child and massage him for a long time with a different oil each night. All this attention pleases him, and he makes sure I know it. At the end of my *defande*, I remove my lovely sheets and leave the old ones there. I secretly pour urine in the corners of the room, creating nauseating odors to disturb Alhadji's senses. I want him to remember my *defande*, for him to feel nostalgic and lament my temporary absence.

Ramla is ever more sad and sullen. She no longer makes the slightest effort, and the more she lets herself go, the more she agitates her husband. I feel our duel reaching its conclusion, and I am already savoring my imminent victory.

Through my brother, I bought several SIM cards without any paper trail. I'm about to play my trump card. Deal the mortal blow! For a little while now, I've been putting the idea in Alhadji's head that Ramla might be having an affair. My accomplices allude to it too, and he's starting to be suspicious and closely monitor his wife. I decide to put my plan in action at the end of my co-wife's *defande*.

At midnight, I put a new SIM card in my phone and call Ramla. When she picks up, I say nothing. I hear Alhadji ask her what's going on. I've managed to ruin her *walaande* and I rejoice at hearing Alhadji rebuke her. I continue to call her during her *defande*. Alhadji is becoming more and more exasperated. And when she claims someone is plotting against her, everyone looks at her wryly.

One night, Alhadji was at the end of his rope. He accused Ramla of having a lover, but she denied it, crying as usual. Alhadji had already had a bad day at the market and so needed no excuse to blow off steam. In a rage, he starts beating her violently, telling her to fess up immediately. She shouts, cries, swears she's innocent. Infuriated, he pulls a long knife out from under the couch and presses it to her throat, threatening her:

"Listen up, you little whore, you will confess right now. Who is that man calling you? You're mocking me, is that it? It's that little lowlife who wanted to marry you, is that right? If you don't tell me the truth I'll slit your throat, and you can trust I won't go to prison for it. In this country, the rich are always right. Confess!"

Frozen with terror, the young woman stammers: "I swear to you that I'm not cheating. I swear on the Quran."

He shouts so loudly that all the house hears and holds their breath. I sense that this time, I've gone too far. If he kills her, I'll never be able to survive. Guilt spurs me rapidly from my apartment. Harouna, one of Alhadji's cronies who lives in the house, is also up and pacing in front of the veranda, distraught. Seeing me seems to soothe him.

"Hadja, he's going to kill her if we don't do something"

I enter through the back door without knocking, followed by Harouna. My heart is beating out of my chest and I'm trembling with fear. We hear Ramla's anxious voice as a drop of blood beads on her neck:

"I swear on the Quran. Bring it if you want and I'll touch it."

"You'll touch the Quran and swear? If not I'll kill you."

I intervene while he's grabbing the Quran from a shelf.

"Alhadji, you will do no such thing!"

"If you meddle in this affair, I'll kill you, too!" he says furiously, turning the blade toward me.

Keeping me at bay, he turns again to Ramla and hands her the Book:

"Here, swear!"

"I swear in the name of Allah and his Prophet that I have never cheated on you," Ramla says, trembling, her hand on the Quran.

"I want more than that," Alhadji continues, his eyes bloodshot.

"Swear not only that you haven't cheated, but also that you will never cheat!"

"I swear that I will never cheat on you . . . as long as I am your wife," Ramla adds at the last moment, a hand still on the sacred Book.

Harouna, who has so far stayed silent, approaches:

"Alhadji, she swore. Leave her alone now. When someone swears on the Quran, there is nothing more to add. Leave it to Allah. Even if you had caught her redhanded, there's nothing more you can say to her, you must take her word for it."

And, full of compassion for Ramla who's shivering and chattering her teeth, I add:

"Yes, Alhadji, let her return to her apartment tonight."

He throws his knife and lets it fall onto the nearest armchair. Harouna confiscates the weapon and puts it in its sheath. Then, saying nothing, he walks out and leaves us alone. That's when I notice the blood spilling heavily from beneath Ramla's pagne. Horrified, I start to scream:

"Ramla, are you hurt? You're bleeding! Oh my God, Ramla, you're bleeding!"

A pool of blood is forming under her feet but the young woman doesn't react. She's still shivering and feverish. Alhadji stares at her coldly and says, angry:

"You're staining the carpet and you've ruined the armchair. You imbecile, that cost a fortune! What's going on? Is it your period? Get up immediately, go!"

"I can't," whispers Ramla, panicked. "I can't, Safira!"

"You're soiling the living room! What are you doing?" Alhadji grows more and more aggravated. "What a disaster, this girl!"

"It's okay, Alhadji. Don't worry. We'll clean it," I say to gain time as his anger intensifies. "Ramla, get up!"

And I lift her with difficulty.

We spent the night in the hospital. I watched over Ramla before her mother took over from me in the morning. Emotion and terror had caused a miscarriage. In the early morning, her pain subsided a bit and she sat up painfully in her bed. I didn't sleep, racked with guilt. I was pregnant, and Ramla, whom I had not suspected was also pregnant, had just lost her baby because of me. I felt horrifically guilty.

I had gone too far. Ramla asked me for water in a barely audible voice and I rushed to serve her. A deceptive calm reigned in this part of the hospital reserved for individual luxury rooms. I whispered in a sad voice:

"I'm sorry you lost your baby. Don't worry, you'll have another soon."

"Who said I wanted one? There's no need to keep up your act, Safira! We're alone. Let's be honest, for once. I thank you for helping me tonight but I know you despise me. I know you've done plenty of things to harm me. I know all about your little schemes. Why? I never did anything to you. I tried to respect you, to be your friend. Why?"

"It's not you I detest, Ramla!" I say honestly. "It's the wife of my husband that I hate. It's polygamy that I . . ."

"But I didn't ask to be your co-wife!"

"In agreeing to be his wife, you agreed to be my rival."

"Who said I wanted to be his wife?"

"What do you mean? I heard so many things about you. People said you wanted to take my place. That you were happy to have finally succeeded after all these years in bamboozling him and convincing him to marry you, when he had always remained monogamous!"

"People say a lot of things, except for the truth! Far from it . . ."

"What do you mean?"

"I'll tell you a secret at the risk of you using it against me. I didn't want to marry Alhadji."

"You'd refuse a man like him?"

"I wanted to marry my fiancé instead. The first man who was granted my hand, whom I loved. We had dreams, plans for the future."

"You were in love?"

"You see! Like you, I had my heart broken the day of the wedding. Like you, I am a victim. I'm just a whim for him. He got one look at me and decided that I belonged to him, no matter what I wanted. My parents also did not take my feelings into account, nor did they listen to my distress. I didn't choose to be your rival; I didn't want to take away your husband."

"I didn't know. I'm sorry. But you are still young and . . ."

"I am no longer young. My youth was stolen from me. My innocence was stolen from me."

"Mine, too."

A heavy silence settles in, each of us nursing our bitterness. For the first time, my co-wife has opened her heart to me, and I discover a sincere, wounded young woman. I break the silence.

"I was wrong, Ramla. Forgive me!"

"It's all right."

"I swear to you that I will never speak to anyone about this, especially not Alhadji."

"I don't care anymore. In any event, I have no desire to be here."

"Don't say that. Alhadji isn't as mean as you think. You just have to know how to handle him."

"What's the point? He's not mean? Not with you, maybe. You love him. You have children, you can tolerate him . . ."

The thunderous entrance of her mother and aunt cuts off our conversation. When they ask what happened, Ramla answers that she fell down the stairs and lost her child. Her subtle wink dissuades me from saying anything more. I confirm by nodding my head and silently receive the warm thanks from her mother for my help.

During Ramla's stay at the hospital, Alhadji did not visit her. Upon her return to the house, he ignored her completely. Her recovery lasted forty days, and not once did he deign to enter her apartment. During that period, I no longer had to share my husband, as if their marriage had only been a parenthesis. But Ramla was still there. After she was healed, she resumed her *defande*. Her uncle Hayatou encouraged Alhadji to have more patience, asking his niece to be better behaved in her home, and then he uttered a wish for none of this to happen again.

VII

S he's gone!"

"What?"

"Last night," my servant continues excitedly. "Apparently she snuck past the guards."

I'm eating my breakfast. It was my *defande* last night and I barely slept. Baffled, I stare at the young girl, unable to believe this news that finally puts an end to my obsession. My heart is racing.

"She fled in the night, leaving all her things," the young girl continues. "They say she also left a letter for Alhadji."

"Are you sure it's true? Who told you?"

"She's really gone, Hadja. And Alhadji is beside himself! He fired both night guards. One of them is my cousin."

I've wanted so long for Ramla to be gone. So why this pang of emotion? Why this unexpected desire to cry? Why this feeling of having lost someone dear to me? I have done everything to chase her away. And now that she's dared to leave, I feel depressed, despondent. I don't answer the servant. Robotically, I abandon my meal and go to Ramla's apartment. I must verify my co-wife's absence for myself. Nothing has been touched. The living room is impeccable. She took nothing, didn't budge any of the furniture. Only a few pieces of clothing are missing from the closet.

Everything else is in order. The vials of perfume, the women's magazine she loved to read, her CDs, everything is there, except for her computer. When did she make her decision? Where did she go?

She spent a lot of time with me yesterday evening. Nothing about her behavior betrayed her intentions. Nothing hinted at her determination. Since her accident and our exchange at the hospital, a friendship had been born between us.

Alhadji, alone in his living room, sips his tea while playing with his remote, switching from one channel to the next. He barely lifts his eyes when I enter. I sit to the side and wait. He continues to ignore me, his face cold.

In the end, I break the silence: "It seems Ramla has left."

"I'm aware."

"Where did she go?"

"To hell, I hope!" he answers, emotionless, his eyes stuck to the screen.

"Maybe she's just sulking. I'm sure she went back to her parents' house or to stay with a friend. Did you fight again?"

I truly hope that's the case and that everything will work itself out. Finally, he looks at me and asks harshly: "What do you care, Safira? You must be happy, no? Your co-wife is gone. Now you're alone again. So stop bothering me about it!"

"I don't want her to leave. Forgive her, Alhadji! She's still young and immature. You have to find her. She can't be far!"

"She's not your wife! She's mine, until proven otherwise. It's my decision. You don't know me at all if you think she's welcome back here. If my wife leaves my house, she has no chance of setting foot here again. But don't celebrate too much. She'll be replaced soon enough," he adds spitefully, to hurt me.

I ignore his last reply and think of Ramla, whom I tormented so much. Her absence already weighs on me.

"Give her one last chance. She's a nice girl."

"Stay in your lane. You are nothing but a wife. It's not up to you to defend your co-wives. Mind your own business unless you want to lose your place too!"

"I like Ramla."

"It's for me to like her, not you. Just more proof that she's not worth the trouble. If she had been worthy, her co-wife would certainly not like her."

Without another glance, he picks up the phone, calls his secretary, and orders firmly:

"Bachirou, are you in the office? I'll be there in a few minutes. Listen up. Prepare me a letter of repudiation for my second wife, Ramla, daughter of Alhadji Boubakari. Address the letter to her father. Tell him that I grant his daughter her freedom, and that she left of her own accord. I repudiate her. Give him my regrets but communicate that it is destiny and the will of Allah, the All-Powerful. Reassure him of my respect and my friendship. Thank him for having given me his daughter. Ask him to send his people to clear out Ramla's apartment tonight. Prepare this letter right away. I will come to sign it and you will deliver it with Bakari as witness."

As he dictates his letter of repudiation, my eyes fill with tears. Without looking at me, he calls his driver and saunters off.

Ramla left before dawn. She braved the dangers of the night and vanished into the wilderness. Several rumors fueled her flight over the course of the following weeks. Supposedly for months she had been in close contact with her brother Amadou via the Internet. He had been working in the capital, as well as with her former fiancé. They say she had also been taking online classes in secret. She took her gold jewelry and is now in Yaoundé with her brother.

With each new rumor, Alhadji's anger intensified. But he was happy to be rid of such an unfit wife. I wallowed in my sadness and guilt. At the same time, I finally had my honor back. I had fought and won—this battle, at least. I had renewed confidence and hope for the future. I had endured polygamy and come out with my head held high. I was no longer afraid of Alhadji remarrying. What had caused me so much pain just a few years ago had now become something banal. Just a parenthesis in the course of my married life, of my life overall. I was convinced that the same scenarios would play out indefinitely. He would marry again, ignore me for a little while. I would grin and bear it and wait for the end of the honeymoon period. After the allure of novelty wore off, his interest in the newcomer would vanish. I would make sure of it. He would end up coming back to me, at least until the next time. I stayed not only out of love, but to protect my children and to be sheltered from need. That was enough reason for me to fiercely defend my place.

Alhadji repainted Ramla's apartment. He quickly hired workers, giving orders for everything, making them start over again if he wasn't satisfied. I recognize that expression of contentment on his face. I know how to interpret his indifference toward me, his eagerness on the phone, his caginess, his ever more hurtful words. I observe his renewed vigor, his determination. Alhadji will soon remarry and, like the last time, I will hear about it through rumors. That's how I'll find out the wedding date, the name of the betrothed, her family, her social status. But, this time, I'll keep my cool. Yes, she will come, but how long will she stay? How long will she last? I am sure of myself and my place now. I will never let anyone take it from me. I am at peace. No matter who comes, I will fight. No matter her weapons, I will still win the battle. The feeling of guilt at Ramla's departure soon gave way to the joy at having my revenge on those who were so smug about Alhadji's transition to polygamy. Although his marriage to Ramla caused me to lose face, any other marriage will be nothing more than the shadow of the last.

No matter what happens, I am the *daada-saaré*. No one will ever be able to replace me. Tonight, I am dressed like a bride. I redid my henna tattoos and asked for the most extravagant arabesques. I put on golden jewels and fine silk pagnes. The day was festive. I chatted and laughed with my friends, exchanged a complicit wink with my sister-in-law and my mother. I also sent my brother and Halima to my favorite marabouts. Herbs, *gaadé*, love potions sit on the highest shelf of my closet. With a smile, I listen to the women of the family harp on with the usual advice, faced with a new bride more brazen than the last and who already shoots me unwelcome looks.

"She is your younger sister, your daughter. It's your duty to educate her, guide her. You are the *daada-saaré*, the foundation of the household. Safira! Safira! You will remain the *daada-saaré*, *jiddere-saaré*. And don't forget: *munyal*, patience!"

ACKNOWLEDGMENTS

The French publication of this novel was supported by Catherine Roger and Françoise Fernandes of the Orange Foundation. I want to thank them first and foremost for their enthusiasm and consideration.

I would also like to express my profound gratitude to Emmanuelle Collas, who welcomed me into her catalogue and warmly accompanied me in the making of this new edition.

Thanks also to Sophie Bagur, France and Justine Collas, and Estelle Roche.

I am grateful to François Nkémé for helping me make this project a reality.

Finally, all my thanks to my husband, Hamadou Baba, who has never stopped encouraging me to pursue my writing, and who offered precious aid in the creation of this novel.

A NOTE FROM THE TRANSLATOR

The Impatient is the story of three women suffering from the same fate: soul-crushing marriages in a country where women have little agency and no escape.

Djaïli Amadou Amal breaks her novel into three parts, one in each of their voices. There is Ramla, who has finally met the love of her life, only to be ripped away from him to be married off to a wealthy and important man in her village—who already has another wife. There's Hindou, her sister, who is forced to marry her cousin, an abusive alcoholic who rapes her, beats her, and subjects her to emotional torture. And there's Safira, Ramla's co-wife, who feels betrayed when her husband of twenty years takes another, younger wife, and who turns to every kind of spell or enchantment she can to ruin Ramla's life. These three women, robbed of their dignity, their control, their ability to experience love in the way they always imagined, are told incessantly to have patience— but these women are fresh out of that.

The novel takes place in Cameroon, and Djaïli Amadou Amal's message is clear: the practice of forced marriage, and forced polygamous marriage, cannot go on. Women must be able to have a say over their own lives, their destinies.

While translating this novel, I needed to find ways to both link and distinguish the three women's voices. They are in a shared, connected pain, they are given the same orders, the same advice, they live in the same village and breathe the same air. And yet, each suffers something specific, and grapples with it in her own way.

Ramla is heartbroken, sad, beaten down, shut off. Her sentences are short and to the point, her language is muted. She observes her co-wife with matter-of-fact statements about her appearance. Because she is resigned to her fate, attempting to stay strong for her sister's sake, I infused the vocabulary and rhythm of her narration with the least emotion of all.

Hindou, the younger sister thrown into the lion's den, is the most frightened, the most helpless. She begs, pleads with her male relatives to help her out of her abusive marriage before her husband manages to kill her. There is more urgency in her voice, but when she suffers the worst atrocities, the life drains from her sentences. When her situation drives her to near madness, she repeats herself, questions herself. *I've changed. They say I'm possessed. They say I'm crazy. They say I'm sick. Have I changed?*

Safira, the jealous co-wife out for blood, is the most passionate, the angriest. She bemoans losing her spot as the favorite wife, she desperately tries to win her husband back. Her narration utilizes the most exclamation points, a frantic charge running through her descriptions, the most domineering word choices, a frequent centering of the self.

And through each of their stories, binding them all together, comes that phrase, again and again: Patience, my girls! *Munyal!*

Emma Ramadan
Providence, November 2021

Here ends Djaïli Amadou Amal's
The Impatient.

The first edition of this book was printed
and bound at LSC Communications
in Harrisonburg, Virginia, in October 2022.

A NOTE ON THE TYPE

The text of this novel was set in Adobe Garamond Pro, a typeface designed in 1989 by Robert Slimbach. It was based on two distinctive examples of the French Renaissance style: a Roman type by Claude Garamond (1499–1561) and an Italic type by Robert Granjon (1513–1590). The typeface was developed after Slimbach studied the fifteenth-century equipment at the Plantin-Moretus Museum in Antwerp, Belgium. Adobe Garamond Pro faithfully captures the original Garamond's grace and clarity, and is used extensively in print for its elegance and readability.

HarperVia

An imprint dedicated to publishing international voices,
offering readers a chance to encounter other lives and other
points of view via the language of the imagination.